THE COWBOY AND THE LADY

A HEATON HOUSE ROMANCE

JANET LEE BARTON

*To Glendell.
I hope you enjoy
Julie's story. Love
your sweet sister,
Janet Lee Barton*

JLB BOOKS

For my Family and my Readers
who love this series and
encouraged me to keep it going.
And to my Lord and Savior
For showing me the way

CHAPTER 1

New York City, 1898

*J*ulie Olsen left the Barge office at the Battery later than usual and headed for the nearest El stop. She was out of sorts and there was no denying it. She'd loved her job when the immigration center was at Ellis Island, but since the fire the year before, it hadn't seemed the same. She didn't know why exactly—nothing about her job had changed.

Maybe it was her life she was unsatisfied with. Ever since Georgia and Sir Tyler's wedding she truly felt as if she should have *spinster* in front of her name. She certainly qualified. Georgia Marshall had been a boarder at Heaton House only a few months when she went to work as a nanny for the widowed baronet next door, and in only a matter of weeks they'd fallen in love.

Over the past few years, Julia had watched first one and then another of Mrs. Heaton's boarders find true love, marry, and move out, only to be replaced by others who did the same thing. At twenty-five, she'd been there the longest and was the oldest of the female boarders. If anyone should feel like an old maid, it certainly was her. Yes, spinster Julia Olson described her well.

And yet, she still wasn't willing to open her heart to just anyone. And it wasn't as if she hadn't had her chances—until she made it clear that she wasn't interested. She couldn't blame her spinsterhood on anyone but herself.

But it was more than all that. With Mrs. Heaton's family coming for a visit from Oklahoma, she'd been reminded of the goal she'd had to go out West—a dream that seemed near to dying now. And why? She'd told herself that it was because her family needed her, and at times they had. But suddenly it hit her that perhaps it was she who needed them. Needed to know they were in nearby Brooklyn while she was living at Heaton House. How pathetic was she—thinking she was so grown up and independent when she'd just let her dream fade because she didn't have the courage to carry it through.

Disgusted with herself, Julia bought her token and hurried up the steps to hand it to the conductor before taking a seat on the El. As she looked out over Battery Park, and then the city with its ever-growing skyscrapers, Julia wasn't sure she could ever leave it all, and perhaps it was time to admit it. She felt at a crossroads of some kind. Only she didn't know which direction to take. Didn't even have a direction in mind any longer.

Well, she'd better get in a better mood soon. Mrs. Heaton's cousin and her son were arriving for an extended visit today, might even be there now, and she wasn't going to put a damper on her landlady's joy.

She got off at the stop nearest Gramercy Park and Heaton House and shored up her defenses as she hurried home.

Because she was the first boarder at Heaton House, everyone else seemed to look to her to lead them, to set the tone. Or at least that's what she believed. And if she was right, she could only set the mood this evening as one of helping her landlady welcome family she hadn't seen in years.

Julia got off at the stop nearest Gramercy Park and headed toward Heaton House. Quietness greeted her as she opened the door. Everyone must be getting ready for dinner. She hurried up to her room and into the bathroom to freshen up. Then she changed into a dressier outfit than she usually wore on a week-night. Mrs. Heaton knew her boarders were tired after a day's work and didn't insist on their dressing for dinner during the week. But on weekends they did spruce up, and everyone was quite happy with the arrangement.

She chose a green silk with an ivory lace inset and then put up her auburn hair, pulling a few tendrils out around her face. She wasn't sure why she was going to so much trouble for people who probably wouldn't notice what she looked like, but one couldn't let herself go just because she was a spinster.

Spinster Julia Olsen did have standards to keep, after all. Suddenly she began to chuckle and then began to laugh outright. Might as well. It was certainly better than crying.

A knock sounded on her door just as she slipped on green tapestry shoes to match her gown. "Come in."

The door opened and both Emily and Betsy came inside.

"We heard you laughing. What's so funny?" Emily asked.

Julia grinned and shook her head. Somehow she didn't think these two younger women would understand. "Just a thought I had. You two look very nice."

"Thank you! We wanted your opinion and to make sure we were dressed appropriately," Betsy said. "We want to do Mrs. Heaton proud."

Betsy had on a blue gown with green trim that she'd made herself. The blue matched her eyes, and she had a green ribbon in her hair. Emily was dressed in deep rose that brought out the gold in her brown eyes.

"You both look wonderful. What do you think? Will I do?" She twirled around, her gown swirling around her feet.

"You look beautiful. Green is your color, Julia," Emily said.

3

"Thank you."

"Let's go down together," Betsy suggested. "I always feel a little awkward around new people."

"You can't be serious," Emily said. "You always seem so confident."

"Only because I don't say much. I just smile a lot," Betsy said. "But deep down I'm really shy until I get to know people."

"Well, I am, too, but I've learned to hide it fairly well." Julia headed out the door.

"You, Julia?" Emily followed. "Why you're always so . . . so composed and friendly to everyone."

"Over the years I've found that if I try to make others feel comfortable, it helps me as well." Not to mention that it helped her hide her own insecurities.

"You're very good at making others feel comfortable," Betsy said. "You made me feel at home right away."

"And me, too," Emily added. "So the trick is so make others feel good. I'm going to try that out tonight."

They were all chuckling as they turned at the landing and hurried down the last few stairs.

Julia turned around to say, "I hope we aren't late." Then she missed the next to the last step and lunged forward.

"Julia!" Emily and Betsy cried at the same time.

Arms, solid and strong, wrapped around her and lifted her before she hit the floor.

"Whoa there, little lady, where you headed so fast? Are you all right?" a deeply husky voice asked.

She looked up, and up, into the deepest, darkest blue eyes she'd ever seen, and a tingling current shot through her veins sending a signal to her brain that said, *Beware!*

"I'm fine. Thank you for stopping my fall, but you can let me down." Several moments passed before Julia insisted, "Now."

❦

4

THE PETITE WOMAN Jake Tucker held in his arms was light as a feather, and he reluctantly put her on her feet as gently as he could. He didn't think he'd ever seen hair quite that shade of dark red or eyes that deep a green. His heart had begun hammering as soon as she lost her footing and he'd hurried to catch her. She was the prettiest woman he'd ever seen, and if he hadn't vowed never to give his heart to another, he'd be happy with the feeling. But instead, he took a deep breath and tried to get his heartbeat to settle down.

She seemed a little shaken as she stood there, probably feeling as awkward as he did. "Did you twist your ankle or—"

"No, I'm fine. Really." She seemed to gather her composure as she smiled at him. "I'm Julia Olsen, one of Mrs. Heaton's boarders. You must be her cousin?"

"I'm Jake Tucker, her second cousin. She and my mother are first cousins, but she's always been like an aunt to me, so I call her Aunt Martha."

"I see. She's been looking so forward to your visit."

"So has my mother. Letters have been flying between here and Oklahoma on a regular basis for weeks now." Much more often than usual, but he was glad for his mother's excitement about the trip. Since she'd given control over the boardinghouse there to his sister, she'd seemed a bit lost and lonely.

"It's good when families are close, even when they live away from each other," Miss Olsen said.

"Yes, it is," Jake replied. "I hope I'm not too early, I was told to meet in the parlor at seven."

"Yes, and you aren't early at all. Come along and I'll introduce you to... Now where did Betsy and Emily get off to?"

"If they are the two women who came down the same time you did, they hurried toward the parlor. I guess they figured you were in safe hands." He smiled down at her.

She hesitated for a moment and then smiled in return. "I suppose so. Come along and I'll make those introductions. We were wondering if you'd arrived on time. I suppose it's a blessing for me that you did."

"I'm glad I was here." Miss Olsen moved down the hall and he followed. "Train was a few minutes late. That Grand Central Station is something to see!"

"You've never seen it before? I thought Mrs. Heaton said you didn't go out West until you were about eighteen or so."

"That's true. But we left from Virginia. Never came up this way."

"That's right. Sometimes I forget Mrs. Heaton had only moved here not long before I became her first boarder."

She smiled at him, and Jake wondered why she hadn't been snapped up by one of the male boarders by now. His mother and her cousin had been corresponding for years, and there seemed to always be news of another set of boarders who'd fallen in love and gotten married. And yet Miss Julia was one of the first boarders. Maybe she was too picky. Or maybe she had other reasons. After all, he did.

They entered the parlor to find the two women who'd come down with Miss Julia...uh Miss Olsen—he must remember his manners and quit thinking of her as Julia—speaking to several men. They all stopped talking as soon as he and Miss Olsen entered the room.

"Everyone, this is Mrs. Heaton's second cousin, Jake Tucker. Mr. Tucker, this is Betsy Thomas, one of our newer boarders, and the lady next to her is Emily Jordan. Betsy is a seamstress and Emily works at Macy's."

He gave a nod with his head to each one and said, "Pleased to meet you, ladies."

"Then the gentlemen are Joseph Clark..." She motioned to a man who seemed a bit older than the others. "He works at your cousin Michael Heaton's agency."

The two men shook hands, and Jake followed Miss Olsen to the next man.

"This is Stephen Adams. He works at the Siegel-Cooper store," Julia said.

"Good to meet you," Mr. Adams said. "Mrs. Heaton has been looking forward to this visit for weeks now. How long are you planning on staying?"

"I'm not sure. Mother has been wanting to come for a very long time, and while we're here, I'm going to try to find out if there is a market for our cattle in the city. I'd also like to look into the mounted police force here. Our city is growing, and we want to be sure our police department is as good as any in the country."

"What about your mother's boardinghouse? She does run one, doesn't she?" Miss Olsen asked.

"She did. But she recently gave ownership to my sister, so there's no timetable been set for us to get back. Mama might never come back this way again, and I'd like her to have a really good visit before we go home." She'd seemed a bit lost after she signed over the deed to the boardinghouse to his sister, Laurie. Running it had become too much for her to handle on her own, but he wondered if she regretted it now. She still had her own room there, and Laurie and her husband Ryan were very good to her, but she seemed unsettled somehow.

Jake had asked if she might want to move in with him, but she didn't want to do that either. So, he and his sister had come up with the plan to bring her to see Aunt Martha, hoping it would cheer her up.

"Well, I think you chose a good time," Miss Olsen said. "Summer will be waning soon, and fall will be upon us."

"Oh, and it's beautiful here in the fall," Emily said.

Two other men came in just then and Miss Olsen introduced them as Samuel White, and Dave Robinson, but before she could tell him what they did for a living, Jake's aunt and mother entered the room.

"Here they all are, Lucy."

Jake's mother and Aunt Martha entered the parlor just then.

"I see you've all been introduced. But you haven't met Jake's mother yet," Aunt Martha said. "This is my cousin, Lucy Tucker, everyone. Gretchen has told me that dinner is ready to be served, so let's get to know each other better as we enjoy it."

Jake held his arms out for the two older women to take and escorted them to the dining room. He then pulled out their chairs for them and rounded the table to the seat Aunt Martha pointed out to him. He was pleased to find he'd be sitting next to Miss Olsen, and he quickly helped slide her chair into place before taking his own.

Aunt Martha's boardinghouse was decorated more elaborately than his mother's, but there was a warm feeling here that reminded him of hers. The boarders all seemed nice and were probably more refined than a few of his mothers had been, but overall, he felt like the family connection had traveled from the East to Oklahoma Territory quite well.

He looked down at the woman beside him. "Thank you for making introductions. I feel a little more comfortable now."

"I'm glad." She smiled at him. "As part of Mrs. Heaton's family, you should feel at home here."

"I have a notion you have a big part in helping everyone feel that way."

Miss Olsen shrugged. "I love Mrs. Heaton. She's like a second mother to me, and I do what I can to see that new people settle in as quickly as possible."

As the two maids began to serve their meal, Aunt Martha said, "Michael and Rebecca and their families will be joining us tomorrow evening. They felt you might be more rested then."

"It was a long trip, and I admit to being a bit tired," Jake's mother said. "But I'm looking forward to seeing your family."

"I'm sure you'll feel better after a good night's sleep, Mother." Jake said.

"Lucy said you have some business here, Jake?" Mrs. Heaton asked.

"Yes ma'am. I'm going to see what kind of market the city might hold for Oklahoma beef. I've got several names of people to get in touch with, and I'll have the weekend free to find my way around before then."

"I'm sure some of the boarders can help you," Aunt Martha said.

"That'd be nice." Jake looked down at the woman beside him. "Would you be willing to show me around, Miss Olsen?"

"Please, call me Julia. We don't go on formalities here at Heaton House."

"Thanks to Mrs. Heaton," Steven said from across the table.

"I want my boarders to feel like family, and it seemed one of the ways to speed that along," Aunt Martha said.

Jake chuckled. "We don't always hold with formalities out West either."

"No, we certainly don't," his mother added with a chuckle.

Jake turned to the woman who he never thought of as a cousin. "I've told Miss Olsen that even though you are Martha to my mother, I can't bring myself to call you anything but *Aunt* Martha."

"I wouldn't have it any other way, Jake," Aunt Martha said. "Your mother and I have always been more like sisters than cousins."

"I'm glad that's all cleared up," Joe Clark said. "I was a little confused there for a minute."

Everyone chuckled, and then his aunt asked Joe to say the blessing.

Jake bowed his head as the man began, "Father, we thank You for this day and for safe travel here for Mrs. Heaton's family. We pray that they have a nice stay, and we look forward to getting to know them. Thank You for our many blessings and for the food we're about to eat. In Jesus' name, amen."

As everyone began to eat, conversation commenced between his mother and aunt Martha, and others at the table conversed between themselves.

Jake leaned nearer to Miss Olsen. "Julia it is then. And please call me Jake. But you didn't answer my question about showing me around."

"I didn't?"

He had a feeling she was trying to turn him down, but he wasn't going to let her off the hook that easily. "No ma'am, you didn't."

CHAPTER 2

*A*s much as Julia wanted to say no, she couldn't bring herself to do so. He had saved her from a falling at his feet, after all. "Well, as it is my Saturday off, I'll be glad to show you around, Jake."

"Thank you. And I'll be glad to treat you to lunch."

"That is very nice of you. I'll take you up on your offer. It's supposed to be a nice weekend. Not too hot for this time of year."

"I look forward to it. I've never been in a city this large," Jake said, taking the basket of bread Mrs. Heaton passed to him. He handed it to Julia, and their fingers accidentally brushed.

The mere touch sent a spark straight up her fingers into her arm to land somewhere in the vicinity of her heart. Not a good sign. She should have told him no and let one of the others show him around.

He was much too good-looking. His shoulders were broad, as if he could hold the weight of the world on them. She'd felt safe in his arms for that brief few moments he'd held her. And he was so tall, she'd had to crane her neck to look up at him when he'd set her on her feet. He was dressed in a suit, but it was a little different from the kind Stephen and Joe wore, probably more common out West. Still, he looked very handsome in it.

Oh, yes, she should have made some excuse not to show him around. Only she didn't want to say no. She wanted to learn more about the West, more about Oklahoma. Who knew, maybe she would actually go to Oklahoma one day. It wouldn't hurt to have a friend to show her around if she did.

"How about a trip to the ice-cream parlor later?" Emily asked. "Jake can see some of the neighborhood at least."

"Would you like to go, or are you too tired from the train trip?" Julia asked Jake.

"I slept a lot of the way. I'm fine, and I'd like to stretch my legs a bit. What about you, Mother? You up to a walk?"

"I think I'd rather stay here and continue catching up with Martha...unless you want to go, too?" Mrs. Tucker turned to Mrs. Heaton.

"No, I'll be glad to stay here and visit with you. We have a lot of years to catch up on."

"Perhaps we should take the long way around to the ice-cream parlor so we can walk off some of this wonderful dinner," Stephen said.

"Now that's a great idea," Joe agreed.

They all lingered a bit around the table and then made plans to meet back down in the foyer in half an hour.

Jake pulled out Julia's chair for her. "Should I change for this outing?"

"I don't think so. We're just going to neaten our hair and grab wraps." She looked over at Stephen and Joe. "Are you two changing?"

"No." Stephen said. "If we change then you ladies will feel overdressed and have to go back up to put on something else."

"And it'll be closing time before we get there," Joe added.

Julia chuckled and looked back at Jake. "Well, there it is then. You don't need to change."

"Good. I'll go down and grab my hat and join you all back up here."

Julia hurried upstairs behind Emily and Betsy, but she'd barely closed her door before they were knocking on it.

"Oh my, Julia, he is the handsomest man!" Betsy exclaimed.

"She's right. And he wants *you* to show him around," Emily added.

Julia shook her head. "He wanted anyone to show him around. No one spoke up when Mrs. Heaton mentioned that one of us would be glad to."

"Stephen and I have to work tomorrow," Emily said.

"And I'm working on Sir Tyler and Georgia's daughters' outfits. We have fittings tomorrow."

"I wonder if Georgia knows Jake and his mother?" Julia asked. "I know she and her family have been long-time friends with the Heaton's."

"She might. We'll have to ask her."

"Yes, but we'd better hurry and freshen up or the men will think we're prettying up just for them."

"Well, aren't we?" Emily asked. Then she laughed and hurried out of the room.

"She is right, you know. Jake Tucker is very handsome. And he certainly came to your rescue. You could have ended up face first at his feet." Betsy said.

Julia shuddered at the very thought. And she didn't want to talk about how handsome the man was with anyone right now. "True. But you'd better get going if you want to go with us. I'm nearly ready."

Betsy grinned as if she could read Julia's thoughts. "All right. But your blush gives you away. You think he's every bit as handsome as I do."

"Betsy..."

The younger girl chuckled and waved her hand as she left the room. "I'm going. I'll see you downstairs."

Julia slipped one more hairpin in and grabbed her light wrap. It wasn't that cool out, but eating ice-cream nearly always made her feel too cold no matter how warm it was outside.

Emily was already downstairs when she got there, and Betsy was right behind her.

As they all gathered, Mrs. Heaton and Jake's mother told them to have a good time from the parlor.

Jake slipped on his hat—a Western type, Julia thought it was called a Stetson. It looked very nice on him, with its tall crown and wide brim. The other men grabbed their bowlers, and Julia couldn't help but notice that Jake Tucker looked more. . . manly in his. At least he did to her.

They all headed outside, and Jake fell into step beside her. They'd only taken a few steps before the door to the Walker House just next door opened, and Georgia and her new husband, Sir Tyler Walker, came out.

"Georgia, Sir Tyler," Betsy said, "we're all going to the ice-cream parlor. Want to come with us? Mrs. Heaton's cousins are in town, and Jake is going with us."

"Jake Tucker? Is that really you?" Georgia came down the steps, Sir Tyler right behind her. "I heard your mother was coming for a visit, but I didn't realize you'd be accompanying her!"

He grinned. "Why yes, it is I, Georgia Marshall. I'm sorry, you're Georgia Walker now. My, you've turned into a pretty woman!"

Julia caught her breath at the too familiar remark, and the look on Sir Tyler's face told her he wasn't impressed with it either.

"Sir—" Georgia's husband started toward Jake.

"It's all right, Tyler. Let me introduce you two," Georgia said. "Jake Tucker and I were next door neighbors before he moved out West. He's like a big brother to me. Nothing more."

"And she was like a pesky little sister," Jake said.

Georgia grinned at Jake. "Jake, this is my husband, Sir Tyler Walker."

Julia felt herself relax a little as the two men shook hands, but she was still unsettled by her reaction to Jake's greeting to Georgia. It felt a little like jealousy, and that wouldn't do. Not at all.

❀

MARTHA HEATON WAS QUITE PLEASED as she settled back in her favorite spot in the parlor and took a sip of the tea Gretchen had just served her and her cousin. It appeared that Jake, her cousin's son, whom she thought of as a nephew, and Julia, her first boarder, had gotten along quite well at dinner. She was glad she'd had him sit beside the young woman she'd come to count on to welcome new people around the table.

She'd been a bit worried about Julia the last few weeks. She'd seemed a bit blue, but when asked if anything was wrong, she always assured Martha that she was fine. She hadn't talked about her dream to move West in a long time, and as much as Martha would hate to see her leave, she wondered if Julia might need a change. It was one reason she'd been looking forward to her cousins' visit. However—

"I love your home, Martha," Lucy said. "And your boarders all seem quite nice. Especially, Julia."

"She's been here longer than the rest and is like a daughter to me."

"I would have thought she'd been married before now. She's quite lovely."

"She is. I've thought the same thing, but I believe she's been disillusioned in the past and she hasn't found a man she can trust with her heart. I do hope that changes one day, for she'd make any man a wonderful wife."

"How much easier it would be if we could pick mates for them," Lucy said. "I thought Jake was going to marry someone not long ago—not that I necessarily approved of her. She was a bit uppity and made me feel that she thought she was a bit too good for my son. But I kept my tongue. Then she up and married someone else and left Jake with a broken heart. Hard as it was to see his heartbreak, deep down I was glad it came before they married and not after."

"I understand how you would be."

"I'm not sure Jake is over it yet, but I certainly hope that getting away and being around other young people will make things easier for him when we go back home."

"They're a wonderful group. I'm sure he'll enjoy their company." From the way he was looking at Julia at the dinner table, Martha was almost certain that Jake would enjoy her company. And Julia had a spark in her eyes she hadn't seen in a while. However, much as she wanted the best for both and wanted them to enjoy each other's company, she didn't want either to be hurt by the other.

SIR TYLER SEEMED QUITE NICE, and he was obviously deeply in love with Georgia. She'd been right, she and Jake were like brother and sister to each other back before he moved out West. Jake was happy for his old friend, married to English gentry. She'd done well for herself—much better than anyone who'd marry him. He loved his life, but he doubted that he'd be able to provide the kind of living these city girls expected—not if he couldn't do it for the one he'd wanted back home.

As they all took off toward the ice-cream parlor, the happy couple fell into step behind him and Julia.

"So when did you get here and how long are you staying?" Georgia asked.

"We got in this afternoon, and I'm not sure how long we'll be here. I want mother to have a good visit. I doubt that we'll be coming this way again anytime soon."

"Do you like it out West?" Georgia asked.

"I love it there. But I'm looking forward to seeing this big city. Julia is going to help me find my way around."

"Well, you can't have a better guide than Julia," Georgia said. "I think she's helped most of us learn our way around."

Jake looked down at the woman beside him, quietly listening to their conversation. "So, I'm not the first one to impose on your good nature?"

"I don't think I'd call it imposing. Besides, you saved me from falling on my face tonight. I think I owe you a favor."

"You don't owe me anything, Miss Julia," Jake said. He didn't want her feeling that she owed him her time. "But I am looking forward to getting out and about tomorrow."

"So what is it like in Oklahoma," Sir Tyler asked from behind them. "I'd like to see more of this new country one day. Perhaps we can make a trip out that way when the girls are a little older."

"We'd be glad to show you around, any of you who might want to come for a visit."

"Why that's very nice of you, Jake," Joe said from up ahead. "Sounds like an adventure."

Jake chuckled. "I can promise you it will be different from what you're used to in the city."

"You know, I've always wanted to go out West," Julia said. "And Mrs. Heaton told me about your mother going out and starting her own boardinghouse. I'd hoped to have gone by now, but..."

"Hurry up, you all," Betsy said from up front. "We don't want the shop to close before we get there."

"We're coming," Julia said. "We should have taken the short way. I haven't pointed out that much to you tonight."

"It's all right. I have a feel for the neighborhood around Heaton House, and you can show me more tomorrow. I have to admit, I think the travel has caught up with me, and if you'd

17

pointed out more, I probably wouldn't have retained much of it anyway."

They arrived at the ice-cream parlor just in time to get their treats, but they chose to take their cones with them, and the owner was quite pleased. He locked the door and put out his CLOSED sign as soon as they all got outside. There wasn't much talk on the way back to Heaton House. Everyone was too busy trying to eat their ice-cream cones before they melted.

It'd been a nice evening. The boarders at Heaton House were a good group, and it'd been good to see Georgia again, but he was definitely looking forward to seeing the city with Miss Julia Olsen the next day.

CHAPTER 3

*J*ulia dressed with care the next morning, not sure why she was so particular about what she was wearing. She always wanted to look nice, but today she'd tried on two different outfits before deciding on a turquoise cotton jumper trimmed in white lace. Betsy had talked her into the style which was new for her. She'd bought a new hat to go with it just the week before, and now the outfit made her feel a little more self-assured.

Still, she was nervous about spending the day with Jake Tucker. She hadn't spent time alone with any man in a very long time and needed all the confidence she could muster. For a moment that morning she'd thought of backing out, but it wouldn't be fair to him, and she didn't want to disappoint Mrs. Heaton.

Julia dawdled for a few more minutes before looking at the clock. She was nearly always one of the first downstairs for breakfast. She'd best hurry or she'd have them all thinking she was sick.

She rushed downstairs and heard Jake's deep voice from the foyer. She entered the dining room and hurried over to the sideboard, trying not to glance over at him. How was she going to spend a whole day with him, if she wouldn't even look at him?

Julia! What is your problem? You're made of stronger stuff than this.

At least she was once. But not so much after finding out the man she was sweet on not long after she moved to Heaton House was a lying, conniving, horrible example of a man.

If not for Michael Heaton, her whole life could have been ruined—and nearly was. Since then, she'd never given another man a chance to pursue her, letting any know before they even asked that she wasn't interested.

She pushed unwanted thoughts of her past away as she dished up some bacon and eggs from the sideboard, added a muffin to her plate, and took her place at the table beside Jake.

"Good morning," he said. "Are you ready to show me the city?"

No. Not with his smile making her feel all fluttery inside. But she'd told him she would, and she wasn't going to back out now. Besides, he only wanted a tour guide. There was no reason for her to be so on guard. He'd made no advances of any kind and was there only for a short time. "I think so. What do you want to see first?"

"I'd like to get to know my way around, find out where the mounted police headquarters are and the places I've been given addresses to so I can set up some appointments next week. I'm not sure it'd be worth shipping our cattle to the city, but I was asked to find out."

"You have addresses or telephone numbers?"

"I do."

"Then that should be no problem. What else do you want to see?"

"I've always wanted to see the Statue of Liberty up close and Ellis Island. Just what most people would like to see visiting the city."

"That doesn't seem too difficult, except I can't show you Ellis Island except from afar. After the fire last year destroyed the immigration center, it was moved to Battery Park, and that's where I work now. But we can look out and see the progress that's been made on the new buildings at Ellis Island. They're set to open in 1900."

"Then I suppose I'll have to be happy seeing it all from afar."

"Take him around Central Park, too, Julia," Stephen said from across the table. "It surprised me more than anything that there was that much open space in the middle of the city. It still does."

"I'll try."

"And don't forget to show him the Park Row Building. Even unfinished, it's already the tallest building in the city," Joe added. "One of our boarders worked on it."

"Really?" Jake said. "I saw some really tall ones on the way here yesterday. We certainly don't have anything like that in Oklahoma City."

Julia wanted to know about Oklahoma City probably as much as he wanted to see New York City. Maybe he could tell her about his home while she showed him hers.

"Will you two be back for lunch?" his mother asked.

"No, I'm going to buy Julia's lunch for taking up her time."

"That's nice of you, Jake. We'll expect you later in the day then," Mrs. Heaton said.

"What are you two doing today?" Jake asked.

"We're going to the Ladies Mile," his mother said. "I've never been there but have heard how wonderful it is."

"My guess is that it's a mile of women's shops." Jake grinned.

Julia laughed at his description. "You could say that. It is mostly women's shops."

"I think I can leave that mile off my list," Jake said.

"I'll make sure not to add it to the list that you really haven't given me much of yet."

"We'll make it up as we go along." He grinned at her, and something fluttered inside sending little tingles of warning up Julia's spine.

Julia jumped up, and Jake quickly did the same, pulling her chair out for her. "There's no real rush. Don't you want to finish your breakfast?"

"I'm full. I'll go up and get my hat, but take your time. I'll be ready when you are."

She hurried out of the room and up the stairs, trying to get those flutters calmed down. What was wrong with her? He wasn't the first handsome man she'd seen ever seen. All the men who lived at Heaton House were nice looking . . . just not in the same way.

Jake Tucker talked with a different accent, kind of long and slow...and deep. And he dressed differently. Today he had on denim pants and a white shirt with a beautifully detailed yoke that made his shoulders seem even broader than they had the night before. He wore Western boots that made him even taller. He looked like all she'd ever dreamed a real cowboy might look like.

But handsome or not, she had to get this—whatever it was he made her feel—under control. Even if he was related to Mrs. Heaton, he was a stranger to her and he'd be going back to Oklahoma where his life was. This reaction she had every time she saw him had to stop. She wasn't...couldn't become attracted to him, and that's all there was about it.

Letting out a large sigh, Julia jammed a pin into her hat. Oh, why had she agreed to show him around? Because he'd asked her and then not let her get away with ignoring him, that's why. She turned and pasted a smile on her face before she swept out of the room and down the stairs. She reached the foyer just as Jake came out of the dining room.

"That was good timing on my part," he said. "Are you ready?"

No, she was not. The last thing she needed to do was spend the day with a man who was way too handsome for her own good. But she had no choice. "As I'll ever be. Now tell me, where do you want to start?"

❀

Miss Julia Olsen seemed a bit out of sorts, and Jake hoped it wasn't because he'd asked her to be his guide. Maybe he should let her out of it. But then what? He needed to be able to find his way around. He handed her a list he'd made while she was upstairs.

Julia looked down at the list and nodded. "I believe I know where these are. One of these restaurants is not far from here. It's early enough you might be able to speak to the owner."

"That'd be nice. You lead the way." Jake couldn't help but wonder why she hadn't followed her dream to go West as she'd talked about the night before, but he didn't feel he knew her well enough to be so inquisitive. Was there some man she was interested in here? Did she have a suitor? Somehow the thought that she might didn't sit well with him, although it was none of his business. He'd never see her again unless she did make it to Oklahoma.

Somehow that thought didn't make him feel one bit better. But he was sure he wouldn't be this way again, and that was fact. He'd try to enjoy seeing the city while he was here, but he was already beginning to feel a bit claustrophobic with all these tall buildings around.

He glanced down at the petite redhead and remembered how light she felt as he'd held her. "But pick the best restaurant for lunch. I'd like to see what their steaks taste like and how they compare to Oklahoma beef."

"That'd be Delmonico's, but it's very expensive."

"And you don't think a free tour of the city is worth it?"

"I—I'm not sure we're dressed appropriately."

"You have a very nice outfit on, and I've never been turned away at a restaurant dressed this way before." Of course, that was in Oklahoma and not New York City. Still, he thought they both

23

looked perfectly presentable. "If they throw us out, I won't sell them any cattle and they'll be the losers."

Julia chuckled. "All right. If you say so."

Her green eyes shone even brighter in the sunlight. It made him think of one of the creeks on his land when it reflected the trees that lined each side of it.

"I do. Besides, any restaurant that'd turn you out doesn't deserve our business."

They went on to The Child's Restaurant, and Jake was happy that the owner made time to speak to him that very day. He invited them back anytime so that Jake could taste his fare and seemed quite interested in finding out about shipping beef from out West. Jake felt quite optimistic when they left.

From there they headed toward Delmonico's, with Julia pointing out another place on his list and other landmarks he might want to check out when he was on his own.

Finally, they reached the famous restaurant, but they didn't even try to get in because it was packed and the line waiting outside was very long. Looking at the clientele, Jake was quite relieved, for Julia had been right. They were woefully under-dressed, especially him, and he could only imagine how embarrassed Julia might be sitting across from him. The last thing he wanted to do was humiliate her. They probably wouldn't have let him in, and that would have been even worse. And yet, she'd been willing to go with him. It appeared she was as kind as she was beautiful.

JULIA WAS glad that they didn't try to get into Delmonico's after all, for she knew she was not dressed properly for the restaurant that catered to the upper-class in the city. Still, she hated that Jake hadn't been able to speak to anyone.

"At least I know where it is now. I'll come back next week to set up an appointment," Jake said as they walked away. "You'll be at work as will everyone else, and I certainly don't want to eavesdrop on Aunt Martha's and Mother's reminisces on a daily basis."

Julia couldn't help but chuckle. She had a hard time even imagining his doing so.

"But I am sorry about Delmonico's. And a little relieved at the same time," he said. "I would have humiliated you by taking you the way I'm dressed. What might have worked back home certainly wouldn't work there. But I will take you there before I go back to Oklahoma, I promise."

"You wouldn't have humiliated me, Jake." The man was much too good-looking for any woman to feel anything but proud to be seen with him. "And there's no need to feel you should take me there. It is very expensive."

"That has nothing to do with it. Perhaps we can go to dinner one night."

"That would probably be even more expensive. And even dressier. I—"

"Julia, I'll probably never come this way again, and I want to go to what is described as 'the finest dining establishment in the country' before I go home."

She tried to ignore the little pang in her heart at the thought that she'd probably never see him again after he left. And she didn't even want to consider why it mattered to her.

"And I am taking you with me," Jake said firmly.

She'd never had any man speak to her in such a way, and she wasn't sure what to say. On one hand, she didn't like anyone telling her what she was going to do, but on the other . . . she'd simply love to go. She'd never been to Delmonico's but had heard descriptions of it from those who had. It sounded wonderful.

"Please...?" Jake asked as if she were about to turn him down.

But she just couldn't find it in herself to say no. Who wouldn't want to go to a fancy restaurant accompanied by him? And it would be a memory she would keep forever, long after the tall cowboy had gone back to Oklahoma. "That would be very nice."

He grinned, and her heart warmed at the expression in his eyes. "Good. It's a date. But I'm getting hungry now. Where would you like to go?"

"Actually, there's a nice little cafe near where I work. It's called O'Brien's. I could show you a couple of other addresses on your list while we walk there and I could point out Battery Park and the Statue of Liberty at a distance, too."

"Wonderful. Let's go."

"But it is a bit of a walk. Are you up to it?" Julia teased.

One of Jake's eyebrows almost disappeared under the brim of his hat as he answered, "Am I up to it? Of course, I am. It'll just whet my appetite. But it'd better be worth it."

"Trust me, it is."

They headed over to Broadway and turned left. "I'm not sure I could ever get used to the traffic here," Jake said. "Back home everyone thinks it's bad in our growing little city, but they'd never complain again if they made a trip here."

"You don't have the El, trolleys, or omnibuses there?"

"No, although there are plans for a trolley in the city. Until then there are lots of wagons, some hacks, and carriages large and small, but nowhere near as many as here. You must take your life in your hands every time you try to cross a street like this."

Julia chuckled. "I guess we get used to it. But one must be watchful because there have been some serious accidents."

"I think being on horseback might be easier," Jake said.

"It that your mode of travel?"

"Most of the time."

"I've never ridden a horse before."

"Never?"

Julia shook her head. "Not ever."

"Do you know if there are any riding trails in the city?"

"As a matter of fact there are. Central Park has wonderful

riding trails from what I've heard. I believe you can rent a horse there, too."

"Hmm, I'll have to check it out."

Julia pressed on Jake's forearm as she came to a stop on a corner street. "Jake, just down this street, on the left, is where the meat market on your list is located. Do you want to see if you can make an appointment?"

"No, it has a telephone number. I'll get in touch with them next week."

They continued until Julia stopped once more. "And over there, on the other side of Broadway, is another restaurant on your list. It's kind of pricy, too. Do you want to set up—"

"No, now you've pointed it out I can make my way back to it. Thank you, Julia. Now we can have lunch and you can start showing me the sights. I think that will be much more fun, don't you?"

Oh, yes, she did. She hadn't expected to enjoy the day, but she'd enjoyed Jake's company all morning. He was easy to be around, and she looked forward to showing him the city...way, way more than she should. "Yes, I think so."

THE CAFE JULIA took them to was nice but not too big or too busy that they couldn't get in. The waiter recognized her and showed them to a small corner table. He gave them menus and left them to decide.

"What do you recommend?" Jake asked.

Julia smiled at him. "I've tried about everything here and usually order the daily special, but it's all very good. It's just plain good cooking and not too expensive."

Jake ordered the Gentleman's Roast Beef Sandwich and Julia ordered a Ladies Lobster Salad.

Jake was enjoying the day even more than he'd thought he

would. Julia hadn't been upset when they couldn't get into Delmonico's and she seemed more concerned with what it might cost him to take her to lunch than she was her desire to go there.

She did want to go; he'd seen it in those beautiful eyes. And he intended to make sure she did before he went back home. He could think of nothing he'd rather do than take Miss Julia Olsen to dinner at Delmonico's.

He might not be worth much in many people's eyes, and he wasn't even sure he wanted to be, but he had built his small ranch from the ground up, one head of cattle at a time. Now the Triple T was becoming known for raising quality beef. He wasn't rich by any means, but he was doing pretty well and his future looked bright...at least to him. He could well afford to take Miss Julia Olsen to Delmonico's, at least once.

Their meal came and Jake took his first bite. "You're right, this is very good. My beef would be better, but not bad at all."

"Your beef?"

"Yes. My ranch is called the Triple T. It's not huge, but my beef is good."

"I—" Julia shook her head. "I thought you were looking into things for your friends. I have no idea what I thought you did, but it never really dawned on me you were a rancher."

Jake chuckled. "Did you think I just helped mother with the boardinghouse?"

"No, but I am such a city girl, I suppose I didn't think outside of Oklahoma City. And truth be told, I don't know much about Oklahoma or ranching either." She blushed a delicate shade of pink.

Jake chuckled. "There's no reason for you to when you haven't been there. Actually, my ranch isn't far from the boardinghouse. It's just outside of town, and while I was putting up buildings, I did live at the boardinghouse. But now I live in a house I built myself. It's not big, but it's mine."

"What an accomplishment, Jake. Your mother must be so proud of you."

"She says so." His grinned. "But she'd be happier with me if I was married and had children."

"And there's no one—? I'm sorry, that's none of my business."

Now why had he said anything about his lack of a wife and children? But he had and he'd answer honestly. "I brought the subject up, and the answer is no. And none in sight. I'm not looking. Mother will have to count on my sister and her husband for grandchildren."

"I see." Julia smiled at him. "At least we have something in common there, and you have nothing to worry about with me."

"No suitor? I find that hard to believe." Truthfully, he found it almost impossible to believe. He'd seen the admiration in the eyes of the men at Heaton House when they looked at her.

"I could say the same. But I . . .no, there is no suitor. And I'm not looking either. I don't trust in men easily."

That was too bad, for she was a delightful woman and very honest. He couldn't help but wonder why she didn't trust men. Had she been badly mistreated by one? He didn't feel he knew her well enough to ask. "Yes, it appears we do have more in common than one might think."

Jake couldn't believe he'd been so open about his personal life. It wasn't like him at all. But something about this woman had him talking to her like she was an old friend. Or maybe it was because she was a stranger that he'd been so open with her. Whatever it was, he'd best be on his guard. He had a feeling Julia Olsen might be much too enjoyable to be around.

CHAPTER 4

*W*hat was it about this man that had her telling him right up front that she didn't trust men? Maybe it was because he was a relative of the Heaton's and she felt he could be trusted.

But how could she have been so candid when her heart had yelled a warning to her the night before, and then again this morning? Several times, in fact. And despite that, she'd been open with him. But now that they'd shared that they weren't looking for mates, perhaps her heart wouldn't be sounding alarms quite so often.

"I'm looking forward to seeing where you work." Jake brought her thoughts back to what she was here for—to show him around the city.

"Are you ready? We can go anytime you are."

Jake motioned to the waiter, paid him for their meals, and then stood and pulled out her chair. He grasped Julia's arm lightly as they left the restaurant and started down the street.

The men at Heaton House were always pulling out chairs for her, so why did Jake doing it feel so different? Why did she feel such a sudden of connection with him? Maybe because he lived in a place she'd longed to see? Or that they both had revealed something about themselves? Whatever it was, she felt more comfortable with Jake than any man she'd ever known. But he'd be going back out West and she must keep that in mind. Until then, she was going to let herself enjoy it for as long as she could.

They walked several more blocks to a park-like setting. A wrought-iron gate with a sign reading BATTERY PARK stood at its entrance. "Here is what we call the Battery. It's served as many things through the years. Munitions were kept here at one time. There was a fort called Castle Clinton nearby, but the fort wasn't used for military purposes. It was given to the city in the 1820s and then became Castle Garden and was the leading entertainment hall in the city. I've heard Jenny Lind performed here."

"Really? When did it become the immigration center?"

"Around 1855 until 1890 when the facility was built on Ellis Island. Then, after the fire last year, everything had to be moved to the Barge office until the new center on the island is finished."

"I'm sure that was awful to see."

"It was horrible." Julia shuddered just thinking about that day. "But everyone worked really hard to get people over here and take care of them."

They walked a little further, and she pointed toward the building she worked in. "This is the Barge office. It isn't nearly as nice or large as the one at Ellis Island was. But the new one will be wonderful."

"Your job must be very interesting."

"For the most part it is. At times it's sad, when people can't come in because of illness or some other reasons, but seeing the joy on the faces of those who are released to make this country their home makes it all worthwhile."

They walked around the grounds a bit further and then over to the railing at the sea wall where Julia pointed out to sea. "There she is, the Statue of Liberty. I know you'd like a closer look at her, but we'd probably want to do that of a morning."

"Even to see her from here is wonderful. She is quite beautiful," Jake said.

"Yes, she is something to see."

"She is that," Jake said. "I would like to get a little closer."

"Maybe we can get a group together."

"That'd be great. I'll bring my camera with me. I'd like to have something to show my friends back home."

Back home. Jake had friends and a life in Oklahoma. It seemed she would have to keep reminding herself that he would be leaving, and she needed to keep that thought in mind so that she didn't get too used to having him around. They strolled around the grounds a bit longer and then headed back toward Gramercy Park.

"We can take the El, if you'd like. I can point out a few other landmarks to you on the way back."

"Let's do it."

They headed to the nearest El stop and were riding up above the streets in only minutes.

"Oh, this is nice. One can see so much more from this vantage point."

"I thought you'd like it." Julia pointed out the Park Row Building that reached high into the sky. "Matthew Sterling, one of our former boarders, worked on it until he and Millicent married. Then he started his own company."

"Matt and Millicent... Aren't they the last couple to get married from Heaton House?"

"They are." Julia smiled. "You seem to know a lot more about us than we know about you."

Jake chuckled. "Mother reads me Aunt Martha's letters sometimes. But mostly I only know about those who've gotten married...for the reasons I mentioned earlier."

Julia chuckled. "I understand."

"So he worked up that high in the sky? I don't think I could ever do that kind of work."

"Well, he probably wouldn't be able to imagine building a ranch either."

Jake threw back his head and laughed. "You're very good for my ego, Julia."

"Well, you know—we all have our gifts. It's a blessing when we know what they are and use them the way the Lord intends for us to, don't you think?"

"I do. And I believe we're happier when we're doing it."

"Yes, so do I. I'm just not sure I've figured out exactly what my talent is."

"You don't know?" Jake asked.

"Not really."

"From where I stand, Julia, your talent is in making others feel comfortable around you and making them feel better about themselves. Not everyone has that ability."

Julia's heart warmed at his words. "Thank you, Jake. You just made my day."

His words had more than made her day, but it was the expression in his eyes that'd set her pulse to racing and she hurried to change the subject.

"There is the theater district," Julia said. Then she pointed out the American Bible Society and Tiffany's at Union Square as the El took them back to Gramercy Park.

"I think I'll have to stay more than a few weeks just to see it all. I have a feeling we've only tapped the surface."

"You would be right."

"You willing to continue to be my guide when you're off work?"

If he'd asked her that this morning, she might have said no. But now she couldn't think of anything she'd rather do. She was beginning to feel she'd gained a new friend, and she was in no hurry for him to leave the city. There was simply no other answer than to say, "Of course I am."

❀

THEY ARRIVED BACK at Heaton House with just enough time to change for dinner.

"Michael and Rebecca and their families will be arriving any time now. We'd better hurry," Julia said as she hurried to the staircase.

"We dress up for dinner on weekends, right?"

"We do."

Jake hurried downstairs and made quick work of freshening up and changing into his Western dress cloths. He'd enjoyed the day in Julia's company a great deal. He'd never felt quit so comfortable in any other woman's company. Maybe it was because he didn't feel she was sizing him up, measuring him against any other men.

After Caroline, he tended to believe that all single women were interested in was how much a man made, what his social standing was, and—no matter what his future might hold—if he could support her in the way she wanted right now. At least that's what Caroline had wanted, and from watching the social landscape back home, it certainly appeared the case.

But Julia seemed different. Perhaps it was because she didn't trust men any more than he trusted women when it came to romance. All he really knew was that he enjoyed talking to her and wanted to learn more about her. And he could, for he wasn't under any kind of pressure to pursue her, and she wasn't attempting to "rope him in," as they said back home.

He slipped on his suit jacket and combed back his hair...to no avail. There was always a lock that wanted to fall over his forehead no matter how hard he tried to train it differently. He slapped some bay rum on his face and hurried out the door.

When he entered the parlor, it was to find that Aunt Martha's family was there and his mother was making over their children. "Jake, come see," she said.

He quickly crossed the room to shake Michael's hand and greet Violet, whom he'd known back in Virginia, too. Then he turned to hug cousin Rebecca, who'd only been about fourteen when he left Virginia. She introduced him to Ben Roth, her husband, and the two men shook hands.

"And these are their children," his mother said, putting her hand on the little girl's shoulder. "This is Jenny, Rebecca and Ben's daughter, and this little one is Marcus. He's Michael and Violet's son. Aren't they adorable?"

"They are that," Jake said. And they were, but he had a feeling his mother's effort to marry him off were going to be worse than ever now. He turned his attention to Jenny. "I'm your cousin, Jake. I knew your parents when they weren't any older than you."

"You did?" Jenny asked. "That's a long time ago."

"It was," Jake said as everyone laughed.

Several of the boarders entered the parlor and greeted his cousins. It was obvious that they were all friends. He liked that about Aunt Martha's boardinghouse. It seemed these people did feel like family. At his mother's, so many were there for just a week or so at a time that they didn't get a chance to get to know each other well before they moved on.

"Did Julia give you a good tour today?" Michael asked.

"She did. She pointed out the places I want to check out, and I know where to go now and how to get there. She also showed me where she works and I got a look at Lady Liberty. I'd like to see her closer up."

"Maybe we can charter a barge to take a group. It's been a while since I've seen it, too."

"That'd be great, Michael. Julia suggested we might be able to do something like that."

"I'll see what I can arrange."

His back to the door, Jake didn't see Julia when she came in, but he heard her voice as she greeted the others. He turned to see she'd put her hair up and changed into a blue dinner gown that deepened the color of her eyes, while the lighting in the room accentuated the highlights in that beautiful red hair.

He made sure to be by her side as Aunt Martha called them to dinner. He hoped he'd be sitting beside Julia again this evening and was quite pleased to find out that he was. He pulled out her chair for her. "You look very nice tonight."

"Thank you. So do you. I quite like the Western dress style for men."

"Why, thank you, ma'am."

They both chuckled, and Jake was struck as how natural it felt to talk to her.

Michael was asked to say the blessing and requested everyone to bow. "Dear Lord, we thank You for giving safe travel to cousin Lucy and Jake. I ask that You bless their time here and let them have a wonderful visit. We thank You for the good weather we're having and for the opportunity to have dinner together with good friends and family. Thank You for the food we're about to eat. In Jesus' name, amen."

As Aunt Martha's help began to serve them, she said, "I've asked Gretchen to provide a picnic meal for us tomorrow. I thought we'd show Lucy and Jake Central Park. What about it? Would you all like to go?"

"Yes!" was the unanimous answer from around the table.

"That's a wonderful idea, Mother," Michael said. "I'd like Jake to know that we do have some open space in this city."

"I'd like to see it, I must admit," Jake said. "I'm amazed at the skyscrapers here, but I did feel a bit claustrophobic a time or two today."

"Well, tomorrow you'll be able to breathe," Julia said from beside him.

"Promise?"

Julia's tinkle of laughter had him smiling. "Yes, I do. You're going to love the park."

"I can't wait."

After dinner, they all gathered back in the parlor and played a few games of charades, which Rebecca's daughter was very good at. It appeared each side wanted her on their team and she had to take turns.

Then Julia left his side to take a seat at the piano and began to play. She played popular songs of the past few years and everyone sang along. "One last one." She smiled down at Jenny who'd joined her at the piano. "What's it to be?"

"You know, Miss Julia. 'Sidewalks of New York,' " the child said.

Everyone chuckled, and Jake and a feeling it was always the final song. Everyone sang with gusto until the last note was played. Then his cousins gathered up their children and headed home.

"See you tomorrow at church," Michael said. "I'm glad you're going to be staying awhile. I think it will be good for both our mothers, and I'm looking forward to visiting with you more."

"I believe you're right. It's wonderful to be around family again. See you at church."

Jake glanced at Julia who was saying her farewells to Violet and Rebecca. She was a very talented pianist along with being an excellent city guide. He looked forward to finding out what other talents she'd been gifted with.

MARTHA POURED her cousin and herself a cup of tea. She'd forgotten how good it was to have extended family around and knew she'd miss Lucy when she and Jake went back to Oklahoma. They'd decided to have a pot of tea together before going up to their rooms. She quite enjoyed talking over the day with someone older, as she was—not that they were actually old at 50. Still, it was quite nice to talk to someone who would be bridging two centuries soon with most of her life in this one.

"I so appreciate Julia helping Jake find his way around and keeping him busy." Lucy took the cup of tea Martha handed to her. They'd gone to the study after everyone went to their rooms. "I hope he'll begin to put Caroline out of his mind and heart."

"Well, hopefully he'll enjoy himself enough here that when he goes back and sees his old love he'll find that his heart is whole once again." At least Martha hoped so. And she was glad that Julia and the others might be helping Jake get to that point.

She'd often wondered why Julia hadn't fallen in love with any of the male boarders, but she'd never shown any more interest in one over the other, and as far as she knew there was no one she was interested in.

She was a wonderful young woman, living and working independently but still taking an active part in her family who lived in Brooklyn. She spent many a weekend with them, helping out in any way she could, as Julia was the oldest and there were six children behind her. Two had recently married, but still, she could see how it wouldn't be easy to make ends meet at times, and Martha had a feeling that Julia helped monetarily from time to time, too. Perhaps that was why she hadn't pursued her dream, feeling that she was needed here.

"I certainly hope that will be the case, Martha," Lucy said, bringing her out of her thoughts. "Right now I'm glad we're staying a bit longer than we'd first planned."

"I am so very glad you've decided to extend your visit."

"Well, Jake helped me to make that decision. He told me that it might be a long time before we came back this way, so to enjoy it much as I can."

"He's a good man, Lucy. It's too bad that young woman back in Oklahoma didn't appreciate him."

"All that is true. I believe money was what drew her to another man. Jake is building a good future for himself and anyone he might marry. But she didn't want to help him build it or wait for the reward to come."

"Then I believe he's better off without her."

"Yes, so do I. I just hope he finds someone who will love him the way he deserves before too long. At least Laurie and Ryan are happy, but they haven't been in a hurry to start a family. I look at your sweet grandchildren, and I must admit that I long for some of my own."

"Don't give up hope. I had almost given up on having any myself, and now suddenly I have two. We have to remember that some things are out of our control, but not the Lord's." Martha smiled over at her cousin. "And His timing is always best."

❦

IT WAS a pleasure to stand beside Jake in church the next morning and blend her alto with his baritone. His voice was so good that Julia stopped singing several times just to listen to him sing.

The sermon was on forgetting the past and going forward, and Julia felt it was meant for her, but she wasn't sure in what way. Promising herself to look up the scripture verse used and study it more, she left church excited about the rest of the day.

When they arrived back at Heaton House, it was to find that Gretchen, whose church let out earlier than theirs, had two huge picnic baskets ready to go and the omnibus Mrs. Heaton had ordered arrived right on time. She'd even invited Georgia and Sir Tyler and his two little girls to join them. Everyone was in high spirits as they piled in and took their seats.

"This promises to be quite an outing," Jake said, sitting down beside her.

"I think you're going to enjoy it." She couldn't wait for him to see the park. It might not be his wide-open spaces like in Oklahoma, but he'd get to see a good bit of sky.

"I'm sure I will...as long as you show me around."

Julia nodded. "I will. I'll even show you where the stables are, in case you want to come riding this week."

"You're a gem, Julia. I'm glad you agreed to be my guide."

"I enjoy being your guide. Who knows? If I get tired of working at the immigration center, I might hire out as a city guide. Maybe start my own business."

"You'd do well, of that I have no doubt."

Julia laughed. "You know, Mr. Tucker, you are good for my ego, too."

"That's what friends are for, isn't it?"

"I believe it is." Something in his expression had her pulse skittering this way and that—not a reaction only friends should cause.

Julia quickly turned her attention to Betsy who was sitting beside her. "How did the fittings go yesterday?"

"Very well. Georgia is determined to make sure her girls are dressed well, especially with Sir Tyler's family coming over for a visit. It was too bad they couldn't make it for the wedding."

"Yes, it was. I hope things go smoothly while they are here."

"So do I."

Julia heard Jake speaking to Sir Tyler and began to relax. Her pulse under control again, she was determined to keep it that way. It was only for that second and truly meant nothing.

When they drove through the gate to Central Park, Jake turned to her. "Now, this is a surprise. It is beautiful."

"This is just the beginning."

The driver stopped at a picnicking area Mrs. Heaton pointed out to him, and Jake hurried to help her and his mother out of the vehicle. The group followed Mrs. Heaton to the spot she'd picked, and the men put down quilts while the women set out the food.

There were ham sandwiches along with fried chicken, potato salad, pickles, and rolls. Desert was a three-layer chocolate cake with thick icing and two different kinds of pie.

They all helped themselves and settled down on the quilts to eat. When everyone was finished, Mrs. Heaton's family, along with Georgia and Sir Tyler, headed toward the carousel for the children, while the rest of the boarders decided to take canoe rides on the lake. Mrs. Heaton and Jake's mother chose to enjoy the shade and visit.

"What do you want to do?" Julia asked Jake. "I can show you the stables and then we can go canoeing with the others or just watch them, if you'd like."

"That's a great idea." He put out his hand, and she grasped it while he pulled her up. "I might like to take a ride or two this week."

"Let's go then."

"You two have a good time," his mother said. "Thank you for showing him around, Julia."

"You're welcome. But no need for thanks. I'm enjoying it myself." She led off with Jake lightly clasping her elbow.

"Now you've done it. Mother is going to be after me to court you." He attempted to appear very serious, but a smile slid on his face.

"Just tell her that we've talked this over and neither of us is in the market for a spouse. I'll back you up if you need me to."

Jake's laugh was so contagious, she joined in.

"Julia, you are a delight! I might have to take you up on that offer."

It was a beautiful day, just the right temperature for strolling through the park, listening to the birds sing and watching butterflies flit from flower to flower.

"I don't think I've seen so many people out and about in my life. But I can see why," Jake said. "If they begin to feel closed in, they can come here and breathe in the air, see the sky, and go back to their homes refreshed."

They reached the stables, and Jake seemed more than a little impressed when he was told how many horses they kept and where the trails were.

"You'll enjoy it, I know," the stable manager said. "Many of our customers are from Europe and from out your way, too. Want a ride today?"

"I'd love one." Jake turned to Julia. "Want a riding lesson today?"

"Oh, I *do* want to learn to ride. But I'm not dressed for it today."

Julia blushed as Jake's appreciative look at the way she was dressed in a slender skirt that would never do for riding a horse.

"You're right. We'll do it another time."

"I'll find something more appropriate by next week. How's that?"

"That'd be great." Jake turned to the manager. "Not today, but I'll be back this week. I can't wait to try out your trails." He tipped his Stetson and turned to Julia. "Thank you for telling me about this and showing me where it is. I'll spend a lot of my days right here during this visit. Now where is that lake?"

"It's not far. Come this way."

When they reached the lake, Julia enjoyed seeing Jake's reaction to it.

"I never expected to see a lake like this in the middle of the city."

"It is one of our favorite places to spend an afternoon in the summer. Look, there are Betsy and Joe."

"And Stephen and Emily are right behind them. It appears like they're having a race."

"Most likely they are. Do you have any place to go canoeing in Oklahoma?"

"We do. There are Lake Overholser, the North and South Canadian River, and several other lakes. Why? Did you think you'd have to row us?" He grinned at her.

"No. But I can if I need to."

Jake laughed. "I don't doubt that for one minute."

He paid for their canoe rental and carefully helped Julia into it. It was nice out on the lake, the breeze cooling the air as he rolled up his sleeves and challenged Stephen and Joe to a race.

Joe grinned at him. "You mean cowboys know how to row?"

"I don't believe it," Stephen said. "Riding horses and canoeing are two very different things."

"I'll show you what this cowboy can do," Jake said as he dipped his oar in the waters. His arms were powerful—one could see his muscles bunch under his shirtsleeves as he began rowing.

Julia grinned and waved at the other two teams as Jake overtook them and made it to the other side of the lake minutes before they reached it.

By the time they turned in their canoes, Jake had claimed three victories to the other two men's one each. Joe and Stephen seemed quite impressed.

"How'd you get your arms so strong?" Stephen asked.

"Riding, roping, and wrestling those cattle is what does it, along with all the other work there is to do on a ranch," Jake said. "Come out for a visit and I'll get you two in shape."

Stephen chuckled. "We might take you up on that offer one day."

Soon it was time to go, so the entire group gathered their belongings, boarded the omnibus, and returned to their homes.

After a light Sunday supper, those at Heaton House thought bedtime should be earlier than usual. Everyone was yawning from all the fresh air and fun.

As they prepared to retire to their rooms, Julia turned to Jake. "I hope you have a wonderful day tomorrow. I look forward to hearing all about it at dinner."

"I look forward to telling you all about it."

"See you in the morning." Julia hurried up the stairs. It'd been a wonderful day, and she knew it had little to do with the weather and everything to do with whom she'd spent it with. But she didn't want to dwell on the why of any of it.

CHAPTER 5

*O*n Monday morning, Jake telephoned the meat market to make an appointment with the manager for the next day to see how to ship to them, should he be successful in getting any interest from any of the leads he'd been given.

Then he took off armed with a map Julia had drawn up for him. It seemed a poor substitute for her company. Still, it was a great help as he retraced their footsteps to the places she'd shown him or pointed out to him on Saturday. By midday he realized she'd given him good enough directions that he was able to find his way to the other places on his list.

Most people had been very helpful if he did ask for directions, although he had run into a few uppity-up city dwellers who looked at his mode of dress and seemed to turn up their noses at him, even though he'd worn his Sunday best.

You'd think they'd never seen the likes of someone like him before, but surely in this city where people came from all over the world, a cowboy from Oklahoma wasn't that much of an oddity. Perhaps it was the Stetson he wore instead of the bowlers most men he saw on the street wore here. Or perhaps his boots.

Then there was the man he accidentally ran into that morning and scuffed up his obviously expensive shoe. Jake had offered to pay for a shoeshine, but the man brushed him off and went down the street calling him all kinds of bad names.

Jake had shrugged it off, reminding himself that there were those kinds of people in Oklahoma, too. Like the woman he'd thought to marry, only wasn't wealthy enough for. One certainly didn't have to live in New York City to be haughty.

Still, he couldn't see himself living in a city like this. Just walking down the streets and having to look up to see the sky made him feel a bit claustrophobic. Maybe he'd go to Central Park that afternoon to breath some fresh air and ride their trails for a while.

By lunchtime, he'd been able to make several appointments for later in the week with the people he needed to speak to at several restaurants on his list. Then he headed back toward the Heaton building to meet up with Michael. His cousin had telephoned that morning and asked him to meet up to have lunch together.

Jake grinned with he spotted Michael waiting for him outside a cafe on the corner.

"You made it, right on time," Michael said, striding toward him. "Seems you did fine on your own."

"Thanks to Julia," Jake said as they made their way inside the restaurant and found a table. "She gave me a map she'd drawn up to remind me where we'd gone, and between that and my memory, I didn't have any problems."

"I told you she was a good guide. Are you going to ride this afternoon?"

"I believe I will. After being cooped up on the train and then walking the streets of this great city of yours, I need to get on a horse and feel the air in my face as I ride."

The waiter came to take their orders and Jake chose a roast beef sandwich so he could sample the meat. Who knew, he might find other avenues to sell Oklahoma beef to besides the places on his list.

Once the waiter left their table, Michael went on with their conversation. "Living here does take some getting used to, I'll admit. But now I don't think I'd want to live anywhere else. Still, I sure would like to come visit you out West."

"We'd love for you to," Jake said. "I'm glad mother and I made this trip, if for no other reason than that we could all reconnect again. I always knew she missed having family around, especially after Papa passed away, and now I realize I have, too."

"So have we. Mother has been excited for weeks at the prospect of your visit. I do hope you'll be staying a while."

"Perhaps. Laurie and Ryan are looking after things for us back home. His ranch is next to mine and I've done the same for them in the past, but . . ."

Michael chuckled. "Depends on if you can take being away from those wide-open spaces."

Jake grinned. "I'll see how I feel after my ride."

"And I'll pray you enjoy it. Having a place to ride right in the city should help."

"I'm sure it will."

Their lunch was out quickly, and they spent the next hour enjoying it and catching up with each other. They parted at Michael's building, and Jake hurried back to Heaton House to change clothes before heading to Central Park.

He arrived back at Aunt Martha's home to find that she and his mother were still out. He was sure his mother was having a great time, and he'd told her he wanted her to have a good visit, after all.

He made quick work of changing and was glad to find the man he'd spoken to the day before at the Central Park Stables. He was on a good mount in only minutes and enjoyed the riding trails even more than he'd expected. It was quite lovely at the park, and be breathed easier seeing the open sky above. He wondered if Julia had been serious about learning to ride and hoped so, for he'd enjoy teaching her to.

His thoughts centered on her while he rode, and again he wondered why she hadn't been snapped up already by one of the boarders. She must be serious about not looking for a mate, for to his way of thinking she could have her choice of men.

By the time he got back to the stables, he'd decided to go to the immigration office where she worked and escort her back home. No need to wait until dinner to tell her about his day. He'd like to hear about hers, too.

***

JULIA'S DAY passed fairly fast, as it always did. Two different ships landed within an hour of each other, and she stayed busy helping with checking the immigrants in. If a woman and/or her children needed to be detained for any reason—their papers needed looked at closer or there was a health problem and they were sent to the infirmary—she escorted them there.

She liked it better when they could get through without any problems, and her heart went out to those who had to be held back for any length of time.

It was these people who'd left their homelands that had given her the desire to go out West, to see something different from what she'd been used to all her life. But she was beginning to suspect that they all had more courage than she did. And she was only thinking about exploring the country she'd been born in, not traveling across a whole ocean to get somewhere she didn't even speak the same language.

Today she was happy that none of the people she'd helped had to be detained overnight or sent back home. As she took off the apron she wore over her clothes and retrieved her purse from the locker assigned to her, she wondered how Jake's day had gone and looked forward to hearing about it.

She said goodnight to her co-workers and headed toward the door. But her heart gave a lurch when she spotted Jake standing near it, dressed in his Western wear and a smile on his face. He tipped his hat as she drew near, causing her heart to flutter.

"Jake! What brings you here? Are you lost?"

He chuckled and shook his head. "No, I'm not lost. I know right where I am due to the great guide I had this past weekend, and I came to escort you home...unless you object."

"No, of course I don't." But she didn't quite know what to think of it. She'd never had a man come to escort her home from work.

"Good." He held the door open for her, and they strolled down the walk to the street. "Want to ride to ride the trolley or the El? Or we can walk if you'd like."

"I get to ride either one anytime I want. What would you like to do?"

"Let's ride the El. I like the view."

They weren't far from the stop and were just in time to catch one that'd just arrived. Once they were settled inside, Julia turned to him. "What made you decide to—"

"To come see you?"

She nodded.

"I wanted to thank you for the map you drew me. I only had to ask directions a time or two, not that I admitted that to Michael when we had lunch."

Julia chuckled. "I understand. And I'm glad the map helped. Did you get to see everyone you wanted to?"

Jake shook his head. "No, not all of them, but I did make some appointments for later in the week. And I'm kind of glad it will be spaced out a bit. Gives me something to do when everyone is at work. I'm not used to sitting around."

"I can see how that would be hard for you. I'm sure you stay busy running your ranch and all."

Jake smiled. "You could say that. My days are long, but they pass fast, that's for sure."

"What is a typical day like?"

"It starts around six, sometimes earlier. I grab a biscuit and some coffee and then go saddle my horse. Then I go out to milk the cow, check on my stock, and make sure they're fed. After that, there's always something to take care of. Mending fences or going into town to pick up supplies and see my mother. She usually feeds me lunch and sends something home for my dinner."

"All that before noon?"

"Usually. Then once I'm back home, I make sure there is hay in the barn, muck out stalls, and take care of the other animals."

"I can see how your day flies by."

"But I love it all."

"I can tell that you do," Julia said, suddenly feeling a bit sad at the thought that he'd be going back to that life soon. She tried to throw it off as she asked, "So what else did you do today besides walking all over the place and having lunch with Michael?"

"I went riding."

"You did? Oh, I'm so glad I showed you where the stables were. I'm sure you could have found them by yourself, but I'm glad you got to go riding."

"It was very enjoyable. Did you mean it when you said you wanted to learn to ride?"

"I did."

"Then let's plan on your first lesson this weekend."

Julia's breath caught in her chest. "You do realize that I don't know a thing about horseback riding."

"I know. But you'll learn, if you're willing to try."

"I'm willing. I'll have to find something to wear though."

"You find it and I'll teach you. I'm looking forward to it."

And nervous as she was about it, Julia found that she was, too.

✿

BEFORE DINNER THAT EVENING, Julia asked Betsy to come to her room to see if they could find something she could fashion a riding skirt for her from. But it didn't take long before she decided there was nothing that would work.

"You'll need something for the apron that goes around the front and enables you to get on the horse and ride looking ladylike all at the same time. Let's go call Elizabeth--she's bound to have something you could borrow, and you're both about the same size."

"Oh, maybe I should tell Jake that I can't."

"You'll do no such thing. We'll find something, if I have to make it from scratch. But it'd be easier and faster to just find something. Come on, we'll telephone her before dinner."

"Betsy, I don't want to impose on you or Elizabeth and-"

"It's not an imposition. I'll telephone her." She paused at the door and looked back. "Are you coming?" Without waiting for an answer from Julia, the younger girl hurried downstairs to the telephone alcove.

Regretting that she'd ever said yes to Jake's offer to teach her to ride, Julia followed, only to find that Betsy was already conversing with Elizabeth on the phone almost before Julia's foot hit the last step.

"I knew you'd help," Betsy said. "We'll be over right after dinner. Thanks, Elizabeth. Yes, I'll tell her." With that, Betsy hung up and turned to Julia.

"What did she want you to tell me?" Julia asked.

"That you are welcome to use whatever she has. She thinks she has two different outfits you can try on, and she said to come on over. And that you can't back out."

Julia only shook her head, feeling a heaviness in the pit of her stomach. Why had she ever said she'd do this?

"It's going to be fine, Julia," Betsy said as Mrs. Heaton rang the dinner bell. "You'll be happy you agreed to take lessons from Jake. Wait and see. He's a nice man."

Well, she couldn't deny that. "He is, isn't he?"

"Too bad he'll be going back out West."

"I'm sure he doesn't think so. I think he misses it."

"Well, we'll have to see he has a good enough time that he doesn't—at least not for a while."

Julia was surprised at the flash of jealousy that washed over her. Was Betsy interested in Jake? "Oh? What do you have in mind?"

Betsy grinned at her. "I said that wrong. I wasn't talking about me or 'us' exactly. I was thinking about *you*. You've spent more time with him than the rest of us have, and he even escorts you home from work."

"But that doesn't mean anything."

"It means he enjoys your company."

"It might mean he was bored and couldn't think of anything else to do." Although she didn't really think that was the case. He'd seemed happy to see her and thank her for the map she'd given him.

"Obviously, that isn't true. He could have gone back to Central Park and gone horseback riding."

"He did that before he came to bring me home."

"Then he must have wanted to see you. Central Park and the Immigration Office aren't exactly close to each other."

"It means nothing, Betsy. Don't be seeing a romance here. He'll be going back to Oklahoma before long, and besides, neither of us are looking for a courtship."

"Humph," Betsy said as if she didn't believe that statement for a moment.

"We'd better get into the dining room or we'll be late for dinner." Julia led the way around the telephone alcove and into the foyer.

"Good evening, ladies," Jake's deep voice said from behind them. "I thought I was going to be late."

"We thought we were, too," Julia said.

"We were making plans to borrow an outfit for Julia's riding lesson," Betsy said.

"Wonderful! That means you haven't changed your mind," Jake said.

"Not yet."

"Oh, she's not going to change her mind once we spend the time to get her outfitted. I won't let her," Betsy said.

They were all chuckling as they entered the dining room. Jake pulled out Julia's chair before taking the one next to her. He leaned near and whispered, "I'm glad I have an ally that won't let you back out."

"Back out of what?" Emily asked from across the table.

"Julia has agreed to let me teach her to ride. Our first lesson is this weekend."

"I think that is a wonderful idea, Julia," Mrs. Heaton said from the head of the table.

"I don't think I'd ever have enough nerve to try," Emily said. "But if you do it, perhaps I'll give it some thought."

"I admit I am a bit nervous, but I have no intention of backing out," Julia said. She couldn't. Not now that the everyone in the boardinghouse knew she'd agreed to let him teach her. She couldn't help but wish she'd told Jake she needed to think about it. But it was too late now, and there was nothing to do but to give it her best.

❀

As it was still light out when Julia and Betsy left for the Talbots, Mrs. Heaton told them that Joe would come to escort them back. Her rule was that her girls must be in a group or have a male escort after dark.

"Thank you Mrs. Heaton." Julia had long ago realized that she had good reasons for those rules and she'd come to accept the offer graciously. They could have walked over to the Talbots, but to give them more time, they took a quick trolley over to the nearest street.

Elizabeth Talbot was one of the sweetest women Julia knew. One would never know that she'd come from a wealthy family and stood to inherit a fortune one day. She'd come to Heaton House pretending to be an ordinary working woman, writing for the *Delineator* magazine. That she and John Talbot, a Heaton House boarder who was a reporter for the *Tribune*, were attracted to each other soon became obvious to everyone but them. From the first, they seemed to rub each other the wrong way, but love had finally triumphed, and they were now married with a child. Little John William, whose name had quickly been shortened to Will, had been born a few months earlier.

Julia hoped their visit didn't disturb the baby and wished once more that that she'd never agreed to the riding lessons. But when Elizabeth opened the door and pulled her inside, she was happy to see her friend whether she could wear anything she had or not.

"I hope we aren't keeping you from baby Will, Elizabeth," she said as her friend whisked her and Betsy upstairs.

Elizabeth chuckled. "Believe me, if baby Will should need me, nothing would keep me from him. But he's sleeping quite peacefully and should continue to do so for a while. John is out on assignment, and I'm happy to have some company." She led them into her spare room where Julia could see several outfits laid out on a bed. "I pulled these out as I think they'll fit you. We're both close to the same size, and if anything needs altered, we have Betsy to do it."

"But I wouldn't want to ruin your clothes, Elizabeth."

"Julia, I don't plan on riding anytime soon, I assure you. Those days have passed. I have John and Will to keep me busy these days, and I wouldn't trade them for anything."

Betsy had been looking at the outfits while they were talking and now handed Julia a plain white shirt and a navy riding habit that consisted of a skirt worn with a double-breasted jacket. "Here, try these on."

Julia slipped behind a dressing screen in the corner of the room and began changing clothes. The skirt had an attached apron of sorts that wrapped around the front to the back where she was sure it attached to something. She slipped out from behind the screen. "I'm not sure what to do with this apron thing, and I know nothing about riding."

Both Elizabeth and Betsy grinned.

"Turn around," Elizabeth said. Then she had Julia look into the mirror so that she could see how she attached it to the skirt, while explaining the why of it all. "It makes it easier to be a modest lady while mounting and dismounting a horse and look quite dignified while riding."

"This one seems to fit you well, but you can try the other, if you like," Betsy said.

"This one is fine."

"It fits you perfectly, Julia," Betsy said. "There's nothing I'd need to do except maybe hem it a bit. It appears a little long for you, but we can let it down again for Elizabeth."

Elizabeth shook her head. "No, this is Julia's now. Do whatever is needed to make it fit her perfectly. But try these boots on with it, Julia. The heel is a little higher than your boots so that you may not have to hem it."

Julia did as directed and was pleased that the boots fit, also. "Oh, that makes a difference," Julia said.

"Yes, it does," Betsy said. "I don't think I'll need to do a thing to the skirt."

"And as for the rest"—Elizabeth reached for a hat—"you'll put your hair up in a bun in the back and wear this, with the veil down over your face while you're riding." She placed it on Julia's head and demonstrated how to wear it.

Julia barely recognized herself in the mirror. She looked kind of elegant. And this was for riding a horse?

"So you've really never ridden before?" Elizabeth asked.

"Never. I've always wanted to, but living in the city all my life . . ." Julia shrugged.

"I understand," Elizabeth said. "I grew up on an estate, and many of the women at Heaton House grew up in the country or in small towns, so they might have learned. But truly, you'll love it."

Julia wasn't so sure, but with everyone helping her so much, she had to give it a try.

"You'll also need these gloves and this cane," Julia said, showing her the gloves and the cane.

"A cane for riding?"

"You need it to help guide the horse from the other side."

Julia began to laugh. "Oh ladies, there is so much I have to learn. I think Mr. Tucker is going to regret his offer within the first few minutes of my lesson."

"No, he won't, and you'll do fine. Why don't you change and come back downstairs? I'll go prepare us some tea and explain things a bit more to you," Elizabeth said. "Just put it all in the dress box and shoe box and bring them with you. I'm so glad everything fit so well."

"Thank you, Elizabeth. I appreciate your and Betsy's help in outfitting me. I would never have known what to wear if not for you two. I shudder to think what I might have come up with!"

Julia and Betsy left the room, and Julia changed back into her own clothes and packed the outfit and accessories in the boxes her friend had provided. Then she took the boxes down with her and joined the two women in the parlor.

Elizabeth poured her a cup of tea and immediately began to launch into explaining how to get on the horse and sit in the saddle. "It's more comfortable than you'd think the first time you see the saddle."

"I'll take your word for it." But Julia was beginning to feel a little less nervous about it all . . . at least for now.

The doorbell rang, and Elizabeth went to answer it.

At the murmur of masculine voices, Julia and Betsy recognized their escorts back to Heaton House had arrived. Her heart gave a lurch when Jake entered the room with Joe. For some reason, she was surprised to see that Jake had accompanied Joe to come fetch them.

There was a flurry of activity as she gathered up her boxes and hugged Elizabeth. "Thank you so much for helping me out."

"You're welcome."

Jake took the boxes from her and then turned. "Thank you, ladies, for helping Julia find something to ride in. Now she doesn't dare back out, even if she wants to."

Even Julia chuckled at his remark. He didn't know how right he was.

Holding the boxes under one arm, Jake managed to take hold of Julia's arm with his other hand as they walked back to Heaton House. She was glad Betsy and Joe kept the conversation going as she was trying to sort what it was she was so fluttery about. Was she nervous about the upcoming lessons...or was it the man at her side that had her heart beating so erratically?

CHAPTER 6

$\mathcal{J}$ ake was surprised at how fast the rest of the week passed. He met with Mr. Benson, the owner of the meat market, the next day. Jake was quite pleased when Benson agreed to his idea of paying him to accept and butcher a head of Oklahoma cattle so that he could give out samples to the New York City restauranteurs.

"With your attitude, I believe you'll be a success, and I'll do well to have some of your beef on hand," Mr. Benson said. "I'm looking forward to trying it myself."

"Thank you, sir. I'm humbled by your belief in me."

The two men shook hands on the deal, and Jake was more than happy when he left the shop with an order for not one, but two of his prime stock of cattle. He hurried to telegraph his brother-in-law and asked him to pick out the cattle and get them on a train. He quickly got an answer that they'd be on the train by the end of the week.

Over the next few days, Jake met with several restaurant owners, managers, and chefs—including M. Grevillet, the head chef who replaced Chef Ranhofer who'd recently retired. He oversaw all the kitchens for Delmonico's. Jake was more than a little impressed with the restaurant as he was shown through to the kitchen one morning, and he was more determined than ever to bring Julia there for dinner before he left.

But he was even more impressed with Chef Grevillet and pleased that the man seemed quite interested in what Jake had to say. He hadn't succeeded in getting an order from him yet, as the chef told him that he only used local beef, but when Jake told him he had some beef coming and offered to give him some choice cuts, Chef Grevillet had finally agreed to try a cut or two after it arrived.

Jake spoke to Mr. Benton and made arrangements to be there when the man butchered his beef. He'd take the best pieces to Grevillet himself.

With all of this going on, Jake still found time to ride and to try out several mounts, hoping to find a gentle one for Julia to learn on. He had a feeling she was more nervous than she let on, but it was clear that the other boarders looked up to her, and Jake was fairly certain she would never let them see it if she was apprehensive.

But he was going to do his best to see that she had a good time and wanted to continue to take lessons while he was there. He wanted to make sure that Julia knew all he could teach her by the time he left to go home.

He'd tried several different horses, and with the groomsmen's help, he'd found a couple he thought would work to start Julia out on. As he started back toward Heaton House after a ride, he couldn't wait until the weekend.

BY SATURDAY, it was all Julia could do to keep from showing how nervous she was about the riding lessons. But she was determined not to back out because, deep inside, she knew she'd be letting herself down most of all if she did. So, she prayed that she'd be able to stay on the horse and not hurt herself or embarrass Jake in the process.

She dressed with care and Betsy's help, and as she went down to breakfast that morning she felt a little daring in her riding habit. Julia was grateful that Elizabeth had gone over how to mount and dismount a horse and given her those tips, but she was afraid she'd already forgotten most of it. And even if she remembered, being told *how* to do it wasn't the same as actually *trying* it. And Elizabeth wouldn't be there to give her pointers.

Julia greeted everyone when she and Betsy entered the dining room but only took some toast and fruit from the sideboard. She wasn't sure her stomach would take much this morning, but she didn't dare give that away either.

"Are you excited?" Emily asked as Jake pulled out Julia's chair for her.

Julia wasn't quite sure what the word was to describe what she felt, but there was no need to show her vulnerability now, not even to herself. "I do believe I am."

"I hope so," Jake pushed her chair nearer the table and took his seat beside her.

"I wish we could come watch and cheer you on," Betsy said. "But that wouldn't be easy unless we were riding with you, and frankly, I have no desire to learn."

At the moment, neither did Julia. In fact, she wished she hadn't voiced her desire to do so. But her dream to go out West had included knowing how to ride a horse. Even if her dream to go out West never came true, she would still like to be able to ride. She smiled over at Betsy. "How about you just pray that I don't break anything."

Everyone around the table chuckled.

"Of course we'll pray for that, dear," Mrs. Heaton said.

"And Jake is a great teacher," his mother said. "In fact, he taught me to ride after we moved to Oklahoma. If I can learn at the age I did, I'm sure you'll have no trouble at all, Julia."

"Thank you all for your encouragement. I appreciate it."

"You'll do just fine," Jake added in a low aside to her, putting her fears to rest—at least for the moment.

❀

BY THE TIME they arrived at the stables, Jake wasn't sure who was more nervous, he or Julia. She'd been very quiet on the way over, and he could almost feel the apprehension radiating off her.

If he felt it, the horse would, too, and . . . maybe he should give her an out. "Julia, you know, you really don't have to do this if you are nervous. We can wait for another day."

"I'm fine, Jake. A little nervous, I'll admit, but I want to do this, and putting it off would only make me more tense."

She had a point there, and he had made sure that Gentle Girl, the mare he thought would be the gentlest ride for her, was reserved for them. *Dear Lord, please let this go well and keep Julia safe. If she gets hurt, I'll feel guilty for talking her into this.* "If you're sure."

"Sure as I'll ever be."

Somehow that didn't give him much comfort, but he asked the stable manager to have the horses he'd asked for brought up and tried to reassure Julia. "We're going to take it easy. I may just give you a few lessons today, and we can come back for a real ride tomorrow or whenever you think you're ready."

"Oh, I don't want to put if off long or else I might change my mind. But I like the idea of my learning as much as I can before we actually go for a ride. Perhaps coming back tomorrow afternoon would be best." She gave a little nod and smiled at him.

Jake was relieved that he'd been able to calm her down a bit. The groomsman brought the horses around and motioned to them to follow him to a small training arena Jake had decided to rent, so that he could teach the basics to Julia. At least he didn't have to teach her how to saddle a horse as that'd already been done for them.

He took the reins of one horse from the man and led a beautiful white mare over to Julia. "This is Gentle Girl. I think you'll be fine on her."

"She's beautiful. But much larger than I was expecting." Julia gave a little giggle.

Jake could tell she was more nervous than she was willing to admit.

Then she looked at the horse he'd be riding. "But not nearly as tall as yours."

"Do you want a smaller one?"

"No, I'm sure she'll be fine. You picked her out, didn't you?"

"I did."

"We'll give it a try, won't we, girl?" Julia turned to the mare who neighed softly and stood still while Julia reached out and rubbed her nose.

Jake turned to the groomsman. "I don't think I'll be needing a horse today. I'm going to give Miss Olsen some lessons today, and we'll make an appointment for tomorrow. Can you ask the manager to do that for us? With the same horses?"

"Yes sir, I can do that."

Jake watched the man lead his mount away and then turned to Julia. "Let's get started. I'll give you a lift up." He led her to the side of the horse. "Can you reach the saddle horn?"

"I'll try."

She barely did reach it, and another groomsman hurried to get a small stool for her to stand on.

"That better?" Jake asked.

Julia nodded and grasped the horn ouf the saddle. "Yes. Now what?"

"Put your foot in my hand, and I'll give you a lift up. Sit in the broadest part of the saddle and face me. Then bend your right knee so that your thigh lies on the saddle and to the right of the upright pommel. Now then, your calf should rest behind Gentle Girl's shoulder with your knee bent. There, that's good."

"It seems a bit odd," Julia said, "but it's not uncomfortable."

"I'm glad to hear it." Jake grinned as he continued to give her instruction. "Now fit your left leg into the leaping head, and I'll adjust the stirrup for you and fit your foot into it."

He adjusted the stirrup to her foot and then looked up at her. "There, that should make the chances of your falling off a little less likely."

"I should hope so." Once she settled in the saddle, Julia released a huge sigh.

Jake couldn't help but grin. "See, that wasn't so bad."

"Not too. Elizabeth explained some of it to me the other night, but it didn't make sense to me until now."

Jake handed her the reins and gave her instructions on how to use them to get Gentle Girl to move forward, turn in the direction she'd want her to, and stop. "Try to relax and hold the reins steady. Firm but not too tight."

She looked so small on top of that horse, he wished he could have just put her in front of him for the first lesson. Had he been at home, that's exactly what he would have done, but these weren't his stock and the park had its rules, and well, so did society. Everything was just a little more relaxed out West than here.

Jake had hold of a lead rein so that he could help control Gentle Girl if need be, and he gave her a few more instructions before saying, "I think we're ready to begin. Hold your reins like I showed you to, say, 'Walk,' and gently press into her side with your knee and she should move forward."

"Walk, girl." Julia giggled when Gentle Girl did just that.

Jake breathed a sigh of relief. By the end of the hour, Julia had managed to walk the horse quite proficiently around the arena several times and then to canter around once with him jogging beside them.

Jake was quite pleased with her progress as he helped her off the horse and set her on the ground. He kept his hands on her waist to make sure she was steady and looked down into her eyes. "You did great, Julia. Do you think you feel comfortable enough to ride tomorrow?"

She nodded. "I do, thanks to you and Gentle Girl."

"I'm glad. I think you'll do fine."

His hands were still at her waist, and she quickly pulled away, reminding him that he'd held her for much longer than propriety allowed, and went to rub the horse's nose. The mare neighed and seemed to nod her head. Obviously the two had taken a liking to one another.

"Guess we'd better turn her in."

"I suppose so. She is a sweetheart."

Jake took hold of the reins and led her out of the arena to find the stable manager and the groom heading toward them.

"Mr. Tucker, Baker let me know of your request for tomorrow, and I wanted to let you know that you're all set for three o'clock tomorrow with the same horses, if that time works for you."

Jake glanced at Julia, and she gave a quick nod. He turned back to the groom. "It does. Thank you for working that out for us, sir. And, Baker, thank you for your help today."

"You're quite welcome, sir. We'll see you tomorrow."

Jake looked down at Julia as they left the stables. "You might be little sore tomorrow, but it should get easier as you ride more."

"I'm sure I'll be fine, and I'm actually looking forward to tomorrow. I was more nervous than I let on today, but with your help and remembering some of what Elizabeth had explained to me, I think I'm excited about riding Gentle Girl again."

Jake was more than relieved that she was.

THAT EVENING, Julia was able to relax and enjoy herself instead of dreading the very basics of just getting on a horse. Mrs. Heaton loved celebrations so much that just the fact that Julia had her first riding lessons had been enough to warrant having her favorites at dinner.

As they all settled at the table, Mrs. Heaton asked Jake to say the blessing.

"I'd be happy to," Aunt Martha. "Everyone please pray with me. Dear Lord, we thank You for this day and all our many blessings. I thank You for helping Julia through her first riding lesson for I would have felt quite guilty for talking her into it had she fallen off. She did quite well and is looking forward to her first real ride tomorrow. Please let that go as well as today. Thank You for this celebration meal we're having, and thank You for family and new friends to enjoy it with. In Jesus' name, amen."

Julia's heart went out to him. Would he have felt guilty if she'd fallen or gotten hurt? If so, she needed to reassure him that she wouldn't have blamed *him*.

"I'm so glad you didn't fall off the horse or anything," Emily said. "Maybe one day I'll have enough courage to learn, but I won't make up my mind on that until you've gone for a ride or two without accident."

"Accidents aren't uncommon when learning to ride, but Julia did very well with her first lesson, and she had a nice, gentle mount," Jake said. "But people do sometimes get pitched off for one reason or the other. A horse might get spooked and take off too fast or might jump over something and lose the rider in the process. Most times the rider isn't hurt that much. The real trick is to get back on after it happens so you can get past any fear you might have."

Julia glanced at Jake only to find his gaze on her. "This is the first time you've mentioned that falling off is fairly common. I suppose you didn't say anything about it before because you thought I might back out."

He grinned. "Maybe. And you still could fall. But you won't

back out now, will you? I'm looking forward to showing you the riding trails in your own city."

Something in his expression had her pulse give a jump and speed through her veins. "No, I won't back out."

"Good."

"Jake, Michael telephoned while you and Julia were out today and said that he was working on setting up an outing for anyone who wants to go see the Statue of Liberty next weekend. I need to get a number for him."

"That is very nice of him. I did mention that I'd love to see it up close. I look forward to it. Will you be able to go, Julia?"

"Yes, I believe so. I'm off most weekends but have to fill in occasionally when one of the other ladies needs time off."

"Well, I'm all for it. I haven't been out there in a while," Joe said.

"I'll have to pass this time, unless we can go on Sunday afternoon." Stephen said.

"Me too," Emily said.

"I'll pass that on to Michael," Mrs. Heaton said. "I'm sure he'll try to accommodate everyone."

"Well, since you two are deserting us tomorrow, why don't we all go get ice-cream later?" Stephen asked.

"Sounds good to me," Jake said. "I have to admit that I do like being able to walk to an ice-cream parlor."

"Would you like to go with us, Mrs. Heaton and Mrs. Tucker?" Julia asked.

Jake's mother looked at Mrs. Heaton. "I believe I'll stay in tonight."

"Yes, I agree," Mrs. Heaton said. "We went to visit Rebecca and Jenny this afternoon for a while and then walked home. I think we'll just stay in and have a cup of tea later. You all have a good time."

"You, too," Julia said.

The group decided to meet an hour after dinner, and once it

was finished, Julia ran upstairs with the other women to freshen up. As she straightened up her hair, she realized she was smiling. It'd been a while since she'd caught herself smiling in the mirror. And if she truly thought about, it had only been since Jake Tucker had shown up.

She'd enjoyed the day more than she thought she would. And she looked forward to the next day. But she had to keep in mind that Jake wouldn't be here forever. He'd go back home, and she'd still be doing what she'd always done here. That wasn't going to change.

But in the meantime, she could still enjoy his company, couldn't she? Especially as she knew they would only be friends. Certainly she could. And she was going to do just that.

CHAPTER 7

*a*fter church and Sunday dinner the following day, Julia dressed in her riding habit once more and again realized she was smiling as she put on her hat and secured it. It felt good to look forward to something again. She couldn't deny that she was still nervous about a real ride, but excitement seemed to be winning out as she headed downstairs.

He really was a nice man. He'd been very gentlemanly when he'd escorted her home from Elizabeth's the other night and then yesterday when he was so patient giving her lessons. She hoped she didn't make any mistakes today so that he could enjoy riding, too.

He was waiting in the foyer for her and smiled when she entered. "You ready?"

"I think so. I mean, I know the lessons you gave me yesterday aren't the same as riding outside an arena, so I hope I won't be too much trouble."

Jake stopped in the middle of the walk and turned her to look at him. The expression in his eyes made her catch her breath. "Julia, you aren't any trouble. I volunteered, remember? And besides, I owe you for helping me find my way around."

"Jake, you don't owe me anything. Anyone at Heaton House would have done the same thing."

"Maybe, but I don't think it'd be nearly as much fun with anyone else as it is with you."

Julia could feel her face flush at his compliment. "Thank you, but I imagine it would."

He just grinned at her and took her arm once more before heading back down the walk. They caught the trolley, and he enjoyed the quick ride to Central Park.

The manager greeted them and had their horses brought around. "Do you want some practice time today, Mr. Tucker?" he asked.

Jake glanced down at her. "Do you feel comfortable enough, or do you want a little more time in the area?"

"I think I can manage as long as you help me get in the saddle and don't ride off and leave me."

"I can't imagine anyone running off and leaving you, Julia." He smiled at her and turned back to the manager. "I think we're fine today."

The groom arrived with their horses and held Gentle Girl still while Julia rubbed her nose. She liked this horse. Of course, she was the only one she'd ever been close to, but Jake certainly did a great job choosing her.

"You ready?" Jake asked.

"Yes, I believe so."

Another groom had brought a step, and Jake went over the instructions before helping her settle into the saddle again. Then he handed her the reins and reminded her which way to hold them to get Gentle Girl to do what she wanted her to.

Once he was on his horse, this one called Midnight because he was so black she supposed, he gave a little nod and brought the horse alongside her. "I think you'll like this trail. It feels as if you're out in the country somewhere, not right here in the city."

Julia was happy when Gentle Girl followed her voice

command to walk and they headed down one of the trails Jake had found while riding during the week. Since the park was the closest Julia had ever gotten to the country, she was curious to see what he was talking about.

It didn't take long as they eased into a wooded area that Julia hadn't realized was there. The trees were so thick it was almost impossible to see the park grounds from there, and she couldn't see any buildings at all on the street side as she and Jake rode side by side.

Then the path narrowed, and Jake pulled Midnight to a stop and motioned for Julia to go ahead of him. "Just do what you are doing and know that I'm right behind you, should she take off unexpectedly. Just stay on this trail. It will widen up in a little while."

Julia felt a quiver of nervousness, but she'd rather Jake be behind her so that he could see where she was, than get lost and him have to hunt for her, so she took a deep breath and gave Gentle Girl a nudge. The horse snorted softly as they passed him by, and Julia couldn't help but giggle. "I'm not sure she likes your decision, Jake," Julia said.

"She'll be okay. But if, for some reason, she takes off in a run, then pull her up as firm and steady as you can but try not to jerk the reins. Just trust her."

Once ahead of him, when Gentle Girl kept her speed the same, Julia began to relax and enjoy the scenery. There were wildflowers here and there under the trees, and it was so quiet she truly felt as if she were in the country.

She turned a bit in the saddle to tell Jake he was right, but her movement must have startled Gentle Girl for she suddenly took off, causing Julia to cry out, which didn't help. She felt unbalanced as she turned and tried to get control, but the horse wasn't giving it back. "Jake!"

"Just stay calm!" he yelled from behind her. "You're doing fine."

Stay calm? How was that possible when you were on a runaway

horse? And what had she been thinking about going out West without even knowing how to ride a horse! What made her ever dream about going to Oklahoma when she obviously was not cut out for that kind of life? Surely any cowboy out to find a wife would want her to know how to ride. How foolish she must look to Jake!

Then suddenly, Gentle Girl veered to the right, and Julia didn't know where she was going-only that she was thankful to still be on the horse as she began to gallop. *Dear Lord, please help me stay on her!*

Suddenly, they burst through some trees and out onto an open field. Julia could only pray that no one was in their path. But it seemed empty, and for that she was grateful.

"Whoa, girl, whoa!" She tried to rein the horse in the way Jake had explained, but she must have heard him wrong for Gentle Girl was having none of it.

Julia wanted to look behind her, but she was afraid she'd totally lose her balance. Surely Jake was still back there.

Then she heard the pounding of hooves behind her and then catch up with her. Jake somehow managed to reach over and grab the reins out of her hands. "Stop, girl," he said in a firm voice.

Now why hadn't she thought of that? Evidently her horse didn't understand whoa! But now Gentle Girl began to slow and then came to a standstill.

"Are you all right?" Jake asked.

"I think so . . . I don't know what happened. I just turned to say something to you, and evidently, she didn't like it.

Jake chuckled. "It wasn't you, Julia. A fox ran across the trail and spooked her, but you couldn't see it because you'd turned. You did more than great keeping calm. You're a natural."

"I don't think so. I feel anything but calm right now—I think my stomach turned upside down. But, it was exciting!"

"For you, perhaps. I was quite afraid she might throw you."

"I'm stubborn. I hung on for dear life."

"Yes, you did, and that's good. Many inexperienced riders would have just given up and fallen off."

"I probably looked a sight bouncing along with Gentle Girl in control!"

❀

JAKE LAUGHED and shook his head. Wasn't that just like a woman? "Julia, you looked fine, but I was worried. Here I'd assured you that you'd be fine, and that fox came out of nowhere! Usually they skitter in the woods if you see them at all. Now you'll probably never want to ride with me again."

"Oh, no. I want to ride again and get comfortable going at more than a walk."

"Well, I did intend to ease you into a gallop when we got to this field, but I think you may have it down pat after today. We just need to work on your ability to slow her down and stop her when you want to."

"Well, if I'd known what the magic word and tone were . . ."

"Tone does have a lot to do with it."

"Do we have time to try it now?"

"Of course. We got here faster than I'd planned, so we have plenty of time." And he was glad she didn't want to turn around and get back to Heaton House as quick as she could.

"Let's start with the walk again and then ask her to trot, or perhaps the cantor would be more comfortable. I've heard the trot can be a bit bouncy for a woman."

"All right."

Jake watched as Julia took a deep breath and let it out. Then she said, "Walk out, Gentle Girl." The horse shook her head a bit and then did as requested, and Julia grinned.

Jake nudged Midnight into step beside her. He loved that she seemed to be enjoying this as much as he did. "Now ask her to canter and give her a nudge," he said.

"Let's canter, girl," Julia said. Again, the horse did as she asked.

Jake congratulated himself for choosing the right mount for this woman he'd come to admire in such a short amount of time.

"Now, tell her to stop in a calm voice and use your reins like I showed you. Don't jerk, just pull up easy."

"Stop, girl," Julia said, following his direction perfectly. Gentle Girl immediately did as she asked.

"Now, you can ask her to walk, canter, and stop, or just walk and stop. I'll follow your lead with Midnight."

They rode around the field several times before other riders burst through the woods and joined them. The disappointment on Julia's face mirrored how he felt inside. "We'll come again, I promise. But for now, we can pick up the trail that will take us back to the stables. It's wide enough that we can ride side by side most of the way and I can give you some tips."

"Thank you, Jake. I can't tell you how much this means to me."

"I'm glad. I hope it means almost as much to you as you showing me around the city means to me."

"Oh Jake, it does. But I think you have a much more difficult job in teaching me to ride than I did showing you around. Like I said, anyone else could have done the same."

But he hadn't wanted anyone else to show him around. Something about Julia drew him to her, and he wasn't sure what to make of it. It was a good thing he'd be leaving for home before too long, for he couldn't deny that he was attracted to the redhead.

But there was no future in that feeling. He'd been burned before and didn't intend to let it happen again. Besides, her home was here and his was in Oklahoma. He needed to tamp down that attraction and quickly.

"I'm glad we've both been able to help each other. And I'm enjoying teaching you to ride very much." More than he'd enjoyed anything in a very long while. It'd be a good memory to take back home. And he was ready to make more before he headed that way.

❧

SUNDAY NIGHT SUPPER was quite enjoyable that evening with Julia and Jake telling about their first ride.

"It was so exciting, if a bit terrifying," Julia said, taking the basket of rolls from Jake and passing them to Emily.

"Now I know I'm not going to try to ride," Emily said. "How in the world did you stay on that horse?"

"She stayed calm," Jake said from beside Julia.

Julia laughed and shook her head. "I don't think I would call myself calm—not the way my heart was pounding along with the beat of Gentle Girl's hooves!"

"Just be glad it wasn't a skunk that jumped out in front of her," Joe said, causing them all to laugh.

"But you liked it, Julia?" Jake's mother asked.

"I did! I can't wait to ride again." She felt better than she had in months. While going out West had been a dream of hers for years, so had learning to ride. She might not ever fulfill the first, but at least she'd be able to ride a horse, thanks to Jake.

"She's a natural. Really," Jake said.

"I think Gentle Girl is just an excellent horse and knows I'm a novice. You did a wonderful job of choosing the kind of horse I needed."

Talk turned to the next weekend when Michael had planned the trip to see the Statue of Liberty.

"We're to leave right after Sunday dinner, so you should be able to make it, Emily."

"Good! I'll have to thank him. I feel I miss a lot of outings, but then again, I do love my job, and at least I live here, so I'll count myself blessed," Emily said.

"As we all should," Julia said. And she was feeling especially thankful tonight. She'd made it through a real riding lesson without getting hurt or disappointing Jake. And he'd promised they'd go again. What a difference a week could make in one's attitude!

And she was glad they'd be going on an excursion to see the Statue of Liberty, for Jake had specifically requested a trip there. But she was a little disappointed that she wouldn't get to ride that day. Still, she wanted him to enjoy it, and it'd be fun to see his reaction to the huge landmark. She turned to him, just as he nudged her arm.

"I'll see if I can get us a time to ride on Saturday. We'll have more time that day."

"Jake, you don't have to—"

"I know. But I want to ride any chance I get, so I might as well take you, too. No telling what kind of ride Gentle Girl will take you on." He grinned, letting her know he was teasing.

Julia smiled at him. "Well, I suppose I might as well go then."

"I believe you should," he said, causing them both to chuckle.

"Should what? What's so funny?" ever watchful Betsy asked.

"Nothing." Jake smiled across the table at Julia. "Just remembering back over the day. You really should have been there, Betsy."

"Well, since we all went our separate ways today, how about we go for a walk later?" Joe suggested.

"Sounds good," Jake said. "Maybe we can stop at the ice-cream parlor. Do you think Georgia and Sir Tyler would want to go, too?"

"I'll telephone and see," Betsy said.

"We had a visit with her this afternoon. Those little girls of Sir Tyler's are quite captivating," Jake's mother said. "And they love Georgia. She's a very good mother to them."

"I think that was another match born here at Heaton House," Mrs. Heaton said.

"And you had a big part in it," Emily said.

"They both needed each other—she needed a job and he needed help. I do not match make, Emily."

"We know you don't, Mrs. Heaton. But if you did, you'd have a great track record, don't you think?" Stephen asked.

Everyone laughed, but there was no denying that many a happily married couple's romance had begun right here in Heaton House. But surely if Mrs. Heaton had been trying her hand at matchmaking, Julia would have been married by now. Instead she was the spinster at the table, and the only person she was attracted to would be leaving for home one of these days.

The very thought put a damper on what had been a wonderful day, but Julia tamped it down. She wasn't going to let it ruin the friendship she had with Jake. Hopefully that would last a lifetime.

Not if he marries someone back home, that little voice that never tired of trying to discourage her said. Only this time, Julia answered with a thought of her own. *Well, he hasn't left yet, has he?*

She was determined to enjoy the rest of the evening. She'd deal with heartache later.

❀

AFTER THE BOARDERS went for their walk, Martha and Jake's mother retreated to her garden out back. Small though it was, it was filled with roses that smelled especially delicious after the heat of the day and the quietness seemed to wash over them.

Once Gretchen brought them a pot of tea they settled at the small table with two chairs in a corner that looked over the garden and the back of the boardinghouse.

"You do have such a different set up here, Martha," Jake's mother said. "I feel I gave a homey feel to the boardinghouse back home, but most people are only there for a short time. They are waiting to get into their own places or leaving to travel to other destinations. Your boarders have made their homes here, and it's obvious you are like a mother to them."

"I feel like a mother to them, and it's what I wanted for my boarders. It's not easy to have a home away from home, especially for young single women who are trying to make it on their own and even help their families out by sending money home."

"Do many of them do that?"

"I don't really ask, but I suspect that some do. I believe Julia has helped her family out monetarily as well as going to help. Her mother was sick for a while last winter, and she spent much of her free time there. Thankfully, she is better now, but Julia checks on her family on a regular basis."

"Where do they live?"

"Over in Brooklyn. We'll have to take a ride over the bridge while you're here so you can see it. Did you enjoy the visit with Georgia this afternoon?"

"I did! I'm so glad to hear that her parents are coming for a visit so I'll get to see them while we are here."

"So am I."

Martha hoped changing the conversation would get her cousin's mind off Julia. She had a feeling that Lucy had her in mind for a wife for Jake—and she would make him a wonderful wife. But unless asked by Julia or even Jake, she was not going to get involved. She had no problem helping things along once it was obvious two people loved each other, and while there was no doubt in her mind that Julia and Jake were attracted to each other, she wasn't sure they were ready to give their hearts away.

Only time would tell what God's plan for them was and if she was needed to help things along. Until that seemed clear to her, she would sit back and watch and try to keep her cousin from getting involved, too. And pray that neither of those dear young people would hurt the other.

CHAPTER 8

On Monday, Mr. Benson telephoned to tell Jake that his beef had been delivered and he was ready to butcher it. Jake told him he'd be right there and hurried to his aunt's study. "Aunt Martha, if you haven't decided on dinner tonight, I'm having some filet mignon sent around later. My beef came in, and I'd sure like everyone's opinion on it."

"Why Jake, how nice of you. I'm sure everyone would enjoy that very much."

"I hope so. I'll see you later."

"Have a good day, dear."

"Thank you. I plan on it. What do you and mother have planned?"

"We're going shopping with Rebecca, and Violet has asked us to lunch afterwards."

"That sounds nice. Thank you for showing mother such a good time."

"I'm glad you brought her for a visit, Jake. We're enjoying catching up."

"I'm glad I brought her, too." For a myriad of reasons. He believed there was a market for Oklahoma beef here, he liked the boarders, and it was great to be around family again. And there was Julia . . . He enjoyed being around her, wanted to know her better, and— He pulled his thoughts up short. Enough of all that. Now wasn't the time to think about all the reasons why or how much he liked her. "Have a wonderful lunch. I'll see you later."

He met his mother in the hall and gave her a hug before hurrying out the door and over to the El stop. He bought his token, gave it to the conductor, and was soon on his way to the meat market to watch Mr. Benson butcher one of his prize cattle and have him cut the choice pieces to deliver to Delmonico's and to Heaton House.

"I must say this is the best-looking beef I've seen in a long while," Mr. Benson said as he cut it up per Jake's instructions. "The marbling in it tells me it's going to taste excellent."

"It will. I'm certain of it. I think Chef Grevillet will be quite pleased with what we're sending him. And wrap up those filet mignons for me and have them delivered to Heaton House in Gramercy Park? Also, could you send several cuts over to O'Brien's and Childs' restaurant and let them know it's from me?"

"I'll be glad to, sir."

"And make sure you get a choice cut to take home."

"Thank you, sir. I'll let my wife know I'm bringing it."

"I appreciate you doing this for me, Mr. Benson. The rest of this one you sell for yourself and keep the other carcass in cold storage. I'm hoping to get an order from Delmonico's very soon."

"Why, thank you, Mr. Tucker. I'll be more than glad to butcher your beef anytime."

Jake tipped his Stetson to the man and left the market hopeful that not only would Chef Grevillet at Delmonico's and O'Brien and the manager at Childs like his beef well enough to order from him in the future, so would Mr. Benson. Word of mouth could do a lot, but tasting the product would seal the deal. He was sure of it.

His next stop was the headquarters of the city's mounted

police division. He'd made an appointment the week before with a Captain Marlow and was quickly shown to his office.

The two men shook hands, and the captain motioned for Jake to take the seat across from him. "What brings you here today, Mr. Tucker?"

"I'm from Oklahoma Territory, sir, and we've got some growing cities there. Before I go home, I want to learn about your mounted division and find out how you use it in your daily police work. I'd like to see if we could make the same kind of program work for us."

"I'll be glad to show you around and tell you about it. But I thought most of your lawmen got around on horses."

"Many of them do, especially in smaller towns, but not necessarily in the city and on our residential streets."

"Do you have time to visit the stables now?" Captain Marlow asked.

"I do, if you do."

"I'm always glad to talk about my mounted division."

The captain put on his hat, and Jake followed him to the ground floor where they headed to the stables.

"We use our mounted patrol in various ways through a day. They can chase a person into an alleyway and make it easier to capture him. They can block a person's getaway or block and divert traffic around an accident."

"I can see how that would be useful," Jake said. "I imagine being on a horse can make it easier for the patrolman to see what's up ahead on a busy street, too."

They arrived at the stables, and the captain took him on a tour where Jake got to speak to several of the officers before they went on duty.

"There's a lot more traffic here than back home. How do you train the animals not to spook at all the different sounds?" Jake asked one of them, named Officer O'Connor.

"We have them trained before we start using them," the officer answered. "Occasionally one will still get jittery, but for the most part we don't have trouble with them."

"A good horse seems to sense what to do in all kinds of different situations," Jake said.

"Yes, it does," Officer O'Conner agreed.

"You seem to know a lot about horses, Mr. Tucker," Captain Marlow said.

Jake chuckled and nodded. "I live in the saddle back home, sir."

"I see. Why don't you come down tomorrow and ride with one of the officers on duty so that you can see firsthand what they do? It'd show much more than we can tell you, and you might get a feel for what they could do in your cities out West." He then turned to the officer. "Officer O'Connor, are you on duty tomorrow?"

"I am, sir. I'd be glad to show Mr. Tucker what we do."

Jake quickly accepted the offer, and after shaking hands with the men he'd met, he took off looking forward to telling Julia about his day.

Once on the street, he checked his pocket watch and realized that he might have time to get to the Barge office and escort her home. That way, they'd have a little time together before dinner. He enjoyed spending time with the other boarders, but Julia was the one who came to mind when he wanted to share what all had happened on a day like today.

He hurried to catch the El and arrived at the Barge office just as she was getting ready to leave. The surprised smile she gave him made it more than worth the hurry to get here.

JULIA'S HEART seemed to do a deep dive when she realized Jake had come to escort her home. She'd been thinking of him and wondering how his day had gone—even as she told herself to *stop* thinking of him.

As she headed toward him, she tried to deny how happy she was to see him, but she had a feeling that the smile on her face gave her away. But his smile reached into her heart, and suddenly she didn't care.

"How was your day?" They both asked at the same time.

Better now. "Not bad," Julia said. "And yours?"

"Actually, it was a great day and even better now that I can tell you about it." He gently grasped her arm and led her outside. "Do you want to ride the El or the trolley?"

"Why don't we just walk?" she asked. If he wanted to talk, she wanted to listen, and there was no need rushing what he had to say.

"I was hoping you'd say that." Jake looked down at her with a grin.

"So what all did you do?"

"First, I went to watch a side of Oklahoma beef be butchered."

Julia squelched up her nose and shuddered. "That doesn't sound very appealing to me."

"I can understand how you might feel that way. But for me— well, it's nice to see a butcher appreciate what we raise out there."

"And I suppose I can understand that. I take it all went well with the butchering?"

He laughed. "It did. I had some filets sent to Heaton House for our dinner tonight, and I look forward to seeing how everyone likes them."

"Mmm, that sounds good."

"It will be. I had some sent to O'Brien's and Delmonico's, too. I'm hoping to have some orders before too long."

Jake sounded quite confident, and Julia found herself looking forward to dinner even more than usual. "I hope you do. What else did you do?"

"I visited the mounted division of the police department, and the captain invited me to go out on patrol with one of the officers tomorrow."

"That sounds like fun for you!"

"I think so, too."

"So you didn't ride today?"

"Not today, but I don't have to ride every day. Besides, I got to ride yesterday with you."

She smiled, thinking back on it. "I'm not sure how pleasurable that was for you. My co-workers wanted to hear all about it, and they laughed and laughed when I told them about the ride I had."

"Do any of them ride?"

"Not that I know of."

"Well, I'm sure they wouldn't have been nearly as calm as you were."

He seemed to be trying to make her feel better about that ride, and she was struck once more with how kind he was. "I don't know if I was calm or just kind of in shock." Julia giggled. "I'm just glad you were with me."

"So am I." He smiled down at her, and the expression in his eyes seemed to turn her heart topsy-turvy.

Julia was going to have to watch herself. This man was becoming very special to her, and if she wasn't careful, she could end up hurt. She couldn't allow herself to care too much for him. He was going back to Oklahoma and the life he had there. Suddenly she dreaded the very thought of his leaving.

He'd become a friend to her, and she had to keep it that way. But she would miss him when he left to go home, of that there was no doubt. Still, she was going to try to enjoy her time with him while he was here. And be very, very, careful to keep her feelings from growing into something deeper than friendship. *Dear Lord, please help me not to fall in love with this handsome cowboy.*

THEY ARRIVED at Heaton House just in time to freshen up for dinner, and Jake met her back in the foyer just as everyone was heading to the dining room.

"Our meal is compliments of Jake tonight," Mrs. Heaton said from the head of the table. "We get to taste some real Oklahoma beef he had brought in. Gretchen told me she'd never seen filets that looked so tender. Stephen, will you say the blessing?"

"If the aroma coming from the kitchen is any indication, they'll be delicious," Stephen said. "My mouth stared watering when I walked in the door. And I'll be glad to say the blessing. Will you all bow with me? Dear Lord, we have so much to thank You for. This evening we thank You for the food we're about to eat by way of Jake. And we do thank him for providing it. And we thank You for this day, for the many ways You bless us every day. We ask that You forgive us our sins, and we thank You that we can come to You through Your son and our savior, Jesus Christ. It is in His name we pray, amen."

Gretchen and Maida came through the kitchen door just then and began to serve them sautéed filet mignon with sauce tarpon and fried potato balls.

"Oh my, this *is* wonderful," Mrs. Heaton said after her first bite.

"What do you feed your cattle?" Joe asked from across the table.

"A good grade of homegrown hay."

"Must be. It's very good, Jake," Stephen said.

Julia took her first bite and chewed the perfectly seasoned, tender meat. It was the best steak she'd ever had. She swallowed and looked at Jake. "I've never tasted beef this good or tender before. It's delicious, Jake. You will have orders coming in soon. I'm sure of it."

Jake grinned at her and let out an exaggerated sigh. "I can't tell you what a relief it is that you all like it. And the cooking of it makes a difference, too. Thank you, Gretchen and Maida, for cooking it exactly right."

"It was a pleasure to have such a good cut to work with, Mr. Tucker," Gretchen said. "Thank you for making sure to send enough for me and Maida."

"I wouldn't think of doing otherwise," Jake said. "I'll have a few other cuts sent over while we're here, too."

"Jake, you don't have to do that," Mrs. Heaton said.

"I know, Aunt Martha. But it's something I want to do. You're feeding us every day. It's the least I can do to repay your hospitality."

"Well, I look forward to cooking whatever you send," Gretchen said as she and Maida went back to the kitchen.

"This is so delicious, I thought perhaps we were celebrating something. Mrs. Heaton loves celebrations," Emily said.

"We'll call it a celebration of Jake's beef making it to New York City. I do believe your beef will be in demand here before you know it," Mrs. Heaton said.

"Well, we'll see. But I thank you all for your encouragement. I'd love to have a market here."

Julia would love for him to also. If so, perhaps he'd have reason for coming back from time to time. The thought gave her comfort. Perhaps their friendship could be a long-lasting one. She prayed it might be possible.

JAKE GOT up earlier than usual the next day so that he could get to the mounted police stables in time to ride with Officer O'Conner. He was looking forward to the day and wanted to be on time. He grabbed a biscuit from the sidebar and stuffed a sausage in it, downing it quickly with a cup of coffee before heading out.

Julia was just coming down, and she greeted him with a smile. "Are you off to patrol the city?"

He chuckled. "I'm off to find out how they do it. You're down a bit early, aren't you?"

"A little. I hoped to make it down to tell you to enjoy your day."

His heart swelled with something—he wasn't sure what—that she'd gone out of her way to see him off. "Thank you. I'm glad I haven't left yet. You have a good day, too."

"Thank you. I look forward to hearing about it all."

"I look forward to telling you." He hoped to get through in time to escort her home again but didn't want to mention it in case he couldn't make it. "I'd best be on my way. Thanks again for coming down early to see me off."

"You're welcome."

Jake looked into her eyes, and the urge to kiss her was so strong it had him catching his breath and backing away. "See you later."

He turned and strode to the door as fast as he could, hoping Julia would just think he was in a hurry to get to the stables and not that he was running away from her. Or rather what he feared he was beginning to feel for her.

He forced that thought out of his mind and hurried to the El. It'd get him to the stables faster.

Officer O'Connor was waiting on him, even had a mount saddled and waiting for him. Jake rubbed the horse's nose before mounting him and turned to O'Connor. "I would have been glad to saddle him, officer."

"It was no problem, Mr. Tucker. It'll be good to have some company on my route." He put his horse in motion.

Jake followed him out of the stables. "Please just call me Jake. I'm used to being called by my first name, or even Tucker like back home. Rarely am I referred to as mister."

"Jake it is then. And you can call me Colin, or just Cole for short. It's what my family back home calls me."

85

The man's Irish brogue made Jake smile. "Cole it will be then. Do you have family here?"

"No. I hope to get them over here one of these days, but for now it's just me."

"So, do you live in a boardinghouse or an apartment?"

"I've been renting a room not far from the stables, but I'm actually looking for a place. My landlady has asked me to move. Her daughter is moving back in, along with her family."

"That's tough. Any idea where you'll go?"

"Not yet. I've been looking in the paper, but what I've seen is either too far away or more expensive that I'd like. Where are you staying?"

"Actually at my aunt's"—he grinned at Cole—"boardinghouse."

"Oh? She wouldn't have an opening, would she?"

"You know, I'm not sure, but I think she may. I'll check with her this evening."

"If she does, my landlady will give me a good reference. What's it like there?"

"I believe that if you asked any of the boarders that live there, they'd say it feels like home."

Cole laughed. "Well, I'm not sure I believe that. It's hard to beat home."

"It is. But I can say that she does all she can to make her boarders feel like they are part of her family."

"Where's it at?"

"It's in Gramercy Park. It's called Heaton House."

"That's a really nice neighborhood. Is it affordable?"

"I believe so. Her boarders are all ordinary working people."

"Sounds better and better. I sure would appreciate you asking her about it."

"I will. And I'll get back to you as soon as I can."

They were riding on Fifth Avenue at a leisurely pace when a ruckus of some kind broke out on the street up ahead.

"Let's go see what's up." Cole nudged his mount into a canter, and Jake followed suit with his, pulling up just beside him as the officer went into action.

Cole pulled a bully club from the side of his horse and began to nudge the two men, who'd obviously had too much to drink, apart. "Hey, hey! There'll be no fightin' on my beat," Cole said.

Jake's attention was on how calmly Cole managed to move his horse in-between the two men and get control of the situation as the men continued to hurl threats at each other. He moved his mount forward in case he could lend support but wasn't sure what he'd do if needed.

Back home, he'd have pulled out a gun instead of a club and hoped the sight of it would serve to calm things down. But possibly not. He wouldn't be the only one carrying a gun, not back in Oklahoma.

In only a few minutes Cole had sent both men in opposite directions, threatening to throw them both in jail if he caught them string up things again. Then he looked out onto the crowd that'd gathered. "Everyone can get back to their own business. No need to loiter."

When the people continued to linger, he motioned with his club. "Go on with you, now."

The crowd broke up, and the two men nudged their mounts into an easy gait as they continued down the avenue.

"If that happens again, is there anything I can do to help out?" Jake asked.

Cole shook his head. "Not really, since you aren't on staff. I'd get into trouble if anything happened to you. But what you did do helped. I saw the men look up as you pulled up beside me. They weren't sure what the two of us might do."

They spent the rest of the morning riding, stopping here and there when a storekeeper came out to visit with them. It appeared that Officer O'Connor had a good relationship with those he tried to protect.

It was more than obvious when they turned the corner of the

next block and ran upon a robbery in progress. A man was trying to wrest away an older woman's purse while another ripped away a bag of food she had in her arms. When they looked up and saw Cole and Jake bearing down on them, they ran off down an alleyway. Cole and Jake took off after them.

Jake automatically grabbed the rope at his side and had it whirling around his head in only a moment. Then he sent it spinning through the air to take one of the men down before he got halfway down the alley. Jake was off his horse and tying the man's hands behind his back at the same time Cole was doing the same thing to the other man. Jake picked up the grocery bag and several cans that'd fallen out.

Cole retrieved the purse the man he roped had thrown away.

"You sure you've never done this before?" he asked as they stood the men up and got back on their horses to lead them back out of the alley.

"Only with cattle," Jake said.

They exited the alley to find the woman being taken care of by a shopkeeper who told them he'd called the station to let them know what was going on. Sure enough a police wagon came down the street and picked up their prisoners.

"Life sure isn't boring around here, is it?" Jake asked Cole.

He chuckled. "I've not had a monotonous day yet."

By the time they rode back to the stables, Jake had a lot of respect for the man. He'd be sure to talk to Aunt Martha about him. Heaton House would be a good place for the man, and Jake was sure he'd fit right in with the boarders.

Cole gave him his landlady's telephone number before he left. "I'd be obliged if you'd let me know either way if your aunt has an opening. My landlady will call me to the phone if you telephone."

"I'll try to find out something as soon as I can and give you a call this evening."

"Thank you, Jake."

"Thank you for letting me tag along with you today. I learned a lot."

They parted ways, and Jake looked at his watch. Julia had most likely left for home, and he was glad he hadn't mentioned coming to fetch her for he wouldn't want to let her down. He'd have to settle for seeing her at dinner and hope that they had some time to talk later. It'd been another good day, and he couldn't wait to share it with her.

CHAPTER 9

*J*ake barely made it back to Heaton House in time to freshen up before dinner, and now he took the stairs two at a time back up to the foyer. He met the others as they were entering the dining room.

He hurried to hold Julia's chair for her, only able to give her a smile and a whisper. "I'm sorry I didn't make it in time to see you home," Jake said before he scooted her forward and then slipped into his chair beside her. "I—"

"How did you enjoy your day, son? What was it like being a mounted policeman for a day?"

Much as Jake would have preferred to share his day with Julia first, he couldn't ignore his mother's question at the dinner table.

"That's what you did today?" Stephen asked.

"It was. And I enjoyed it a great deal. It was quite interesting to see how these officers can keep order on a horse. They really are a commanding presence on the streets."

"So, what exactly do the mounted police do besides ride up and down the streets?"

"They break up fights that build up. We came upon a brawl first thing this morning that took some maneuvering on the part of the officer to break up. They also get to know all the shop-keepers and residents along their routes. And they get reports of theft or suspicious characters from them and residents in the neighborhoods they patrol."

"Sounds like quite an interesting day," Julia said from beside him.

"It was. And Aunt Martha, the officer I rode with is named Colin O'Connor. He's a nice man, but he's in need of a place to stay. I wonder—I've never asked about how many rooms you have available downstairs, but—"

"As a matter of fact, I have a couple of open rooms for men. Would you recommend him?"

"After spending all day with him, I would. I told him I'd check with you and let him know as soon as possible."

"Well, tell him I do have a room available and will be glad to meet with him to see if it suits him."

"I'll telephone him right after dinner. Thank you, Aunt Martha."

"Thank you, Jake. I'd been thinking of putting out my sign again but didn't want to deal with it all while you and Lucy are visiting. Thanks to you I won't have to."

"I think you'll all like him. He's a good man."

JULIA HAD BEEN DISAPPOINTED NOT to see Jake when she had gotten off work, but she'd told herself it was for the best. The last thing she needed was to get accustomed to his escorting her home each day. But he'd been so sweet to apologize for some-thing he didn't have to do at all, and now that she'd heard about his day, she certainly understood that he hadn't had time. But he'd intended to, and knowing that lifted her mood like a bird taking flight.

"So what is this officer really like?" Emily asked, bringing them back to the present.

"He's very likable," Jake said. "He's from Ireland and has no family here. I told him that everyone feels like family at Heaton House."

"That's certainly true," Betsy said. "I can't imagine living anywhere else."

"I think you'll all like him. And I felt sorry for him, having no family around. His landlady's daughter is moving back, and she needs the room he rents. So, he has to do something soon."

"I'm glad you met him today," Julia said. "I always wonder what it's like for those immigrants who have no family to meet them and don't know anyone. Most come in as families, but not all."

"We'll make him feel one of us, should he and Mrs. Heaton come to an agreement," Stephen said.

"That's what I love about you all. You truly do help make newcomers feel welcome," Mrs. Heaton said. "And Julia, you of course have set that tone by doing so from the very first."

"But I learned that from your example, Mrs. Heaton."

"That is sweet of you to say, dear," her landlady said.

"Anyone up for a walk tonight?" Jake asked as everyone finished up their meals. "It's nice out."

"It is that. I'll go," Julia said as others around the table agreed to the plan. She hoped she and Jake might have a little time together to talk, but with the whole group going, she doubted it. However, when she came back down after freshening up later, it was to find that Jake had sent the rest of them on their way.

"I was still talking to O'Connor to let him know he had a room if he wants it and told them we'd catch up," he said as he grabbed his Stetson off the rack in the foyer.

"Good. I was hoping to hear more about your day."

"There's not a lot more to tell, except that I truly did enjoy it. I'd never thought of all the ways a mounted patrol would enhance a police presence until I saw it all in action. And a galloping horse can get through traffic and tight spaces much faster than a running man. I think I'd enjoy the job as much as Cole seemed to. He was very excited about the open room and said that he'll be coming by to see Aunt Martha tomorrow."

"Cole? Is that Mr. O'Connor's name?

"Collin, but he said his family calls him Cole."

"I hope things work out for him to rent from Mrs. Heaton. Sounds like he needs friends."

"He probably does have a few, but I got the impression that he's the only boarder in the place he's at."

"Well, Heaton House will be a nice change for him. And everyone will help him settle in."

"So, how was your day?"

"It was good. Not many detentions and so many excited to begin their lives here. You know it's those going out West that have always caught my attention. I've only ever lived in Brooklyn and here."

"Well, it's certainly different out West. Life is a bit slower there. It might be hard to get used to at first." He shrugged. "But there seems to be a lot of the same things going on there, only on a much smaller scale than this city. But those who planned for the land run back in '89 did it well. The cities were laid out in a practical way, and everything grew very fast. The city planners were prepared for families who wanted the things they were used to available there quickly."

"What do you mean?"

"We have parks, the theater, restaurants, shopping, and pretty much all the things people here would want if they up and moved."

"Hey, you two, are you going to catch up with us or not?" Betsy called from up ahead.

"Yes, we're coming," Julia replied.

"We should have waited a few more minutes before setting out. They must have been dawdling, waiting on us," Jake said.

He sounded a little disappointed as they hurried their steps to catch up with the group.

Julia was glad she wasn't the only one that felt that way. There never seemed to be enough time to carry on a really good conversation between the two of them, leaving Julia always wising for more.

"I'm going to make sure to be on time tomorrow to escort you home, and I'd like to walk, if it's all right with you," Jake said.

Julia's frustration with the situation eased. "It is fine with me. I'd like that, too."

Jake gave a short nod as they came nearer to the others. "Good. I'm looking forward to it."

❦

WHEN JAKE HEARD the voice on the other end of the line, he was quite happy to have been called away from the breakfast table the next morning.

"Mr. Tucker, this is Chef Grevillet at Delmonico's. I wanted to thank you for having those special cuts of your beef sent over. I wonder if you'd like to meet with me to discuss your price on the occasional order?"

"Certainly. What time would be best for you?"

"Mornings are best. Could you be here in an hour or so?"

"I can."

"Good. I'll see you then."

Jake hurried back to the dining room with the news.

"Jake, that's wonderful!" Julia was the first to say.

"Well, he did say an *occasional* order. But I'm hoping his customers will soon change that to regular. Of course, that all depends on how this meeting goes. Wish me well."

"Of course we do," Julia said.

"I can't wait to hear what he has to say," Aunt Martha said. "I think this may call for another celebration!"

"Let's see what happens first," Jake said. But he was hopeful there would be cause for celebration.

His hope held as Chef Grevillet welcomed him into his office just off the kitchen of Delmonico's.

"I served your beef to the owner and to some of our special guests last evening. I've been given the go-ahead to order from you what I think I can sell, if your price is right."

"What are you thinking of ordering?"

"Well, I thought I'd go for a couple of head of cattle at a time, once a month to start? We'll see how it goes over before I change that."

Two a month was more than he'd thought it might be. Jake tried not to show how pleased he was. He didn't want the chef to have the upper hand in this deal. "I'd be open to that for now."

Jake was more than satisfied with the agreement they came to when he left Delmonico's, and he believed there'd be more orders to come. He telegraphed home to let them know to ship two more cattle out. Then he went to the meat market to have more meat sent to Heaton House. If not tonight, they would certainly celebrate the next.

He couldn't wait to tell Julia about the deal, but he'd have to wait until she got off work. In the meantime, he decided to go back to Heaton House to see if Cole had been there yet. He'd said it was his day off, and if he decided to move, Jake could help him with it.

He arrived back just as Cole and Mrs. Heaton were sealing the deal. After thanking Jake for mentioning the boardinghouse, the officer also took him up on his offer to help move. He'd be eating dinner and sleeping at Heaton House that night.

"Again, I can't thank you enough, Jake," Cole said as they left to pack up his belongings. "I felt at home the moment I walked in the door and Mrs. Heaton greeted me. She is everything you said she was, and I look forward to meeting everyone this evening."

"I think they're all looking forward to welcoming you."

Cole didn't have a lot to move, and they made quick work of it. He handed in his key to his landlady, and she thanked him for being a good boarder and wished him well. Then they were on their way back to Heaton House.

Aunt Martha had already given him a key to his room, which was just across from Jake's room. They entered and set the cases they'd carried on the bed.

Jake turned to the door. "I'll leave you to settle in. I've got something I must do, but I'll be back before dinner. We meet upstairs in the parlor."

"Yes, Mrs. Heaton explained it to me. It'll be nice to have people to talk to during meals. My landlady was a woman of few words. I'll see you later. Thank you again."

"You're welcome. But I have a feeling the Lord had a lot to do with our meeting and this coming about. He deserves the credit for it."

"I believe you're right. I'll be thanking Him in my prayers for days to come."

"See you later." Jake hurried back upstairs as the clock chimed the half-hour. He had just enough time to meet up with Julia.

She was just walking outside when he arrived. "I thought perhaps you'd been delayed again."

"Cole moved in today and I helped him move his things and that made me later than I wanted, but I was determined to get here in time."

"And you did. I'm glad."

"So am I." He took her arm, and they headed down the street.

"I'm sure Cole will be happy at Heaton House. Everyone will make him feel at home," Julia said.

"I have no doubt of that. I'm glad Aunt Martha had a room for him."

"So am I. How did your meeting go with the chef?" Julia asked.

"Better than I expected." He told her about the agreement he and the chef had come to.

"Jake, I'm so happy for you!"

And she was. He could see it in her eyes. Why had this woman not been snapped up by now? She was everything a man could ask for and more. He had to know. "Julia, I know I may be over-stepping the bounds of our friendship, and you can tell me this is none of my business, but why have you never married?" He half expected her to dress him down for even asking, but she didn't.

"It's not as if I never planned to. It's just that I fell for the wrong man when I first moved to Heaton House, and well, he wasn't trustworthy and I almost—"

"Did he try to—" Jake didn't know how to ask what was in his mind delicately. But he had to know. "Did he force himself on you?"

"No. But he led me on and even had me sneaking out of Heaton House against Mrs. Heaton's rules. Rules that I fully understand why she has in place now. He wasn't a good influence on me, although I should have realized that from the first and been stronger. I can't lay all the blame on him."

"Julia, he never should have encouraged you to sneak out or—"

"I was raised better, Jake. My only excuse is that I thought he loved me and wanted to marry me, but it turned out that he was the most dishonest, immoral man I've ever met. Thankfully Michael realized I was sneaking out and investigated him without my knowledge. He found out he was married--had been for over four years and even had two children. He saved me from making an awful mistake. And he never told his mother that I'd broken her rules. I ended up confessing it all to her and asking her forgiveness, and she gave me even more than that. She gave me a shoulder to cry on. I'm truly beholden to Michael and his mother."

Jake breathed a sigh of relief that Michael found out about the man before Julia had ruined her life. But the consequences of it all saddened him. "And now you don't trust any man?"

"I've been careful not to let myself care enough for one to need to trust him. Why, when I can't trust my own judgement?"

He understood. How could he not after Caroline? Still, he was furious with a man he'd never met for trying to deceive Julia and more than a little surprised at the disappointment he felt about her decision never to fall in love again. "I'm sorry you had to go through all that, but surely you know all men aren't like that."

"I do. Still, as I said, it's my own judgement I'm in doubt of. But now it's my turn. Why have *you* decided never to marry?"

Jake shrugged. Turnabout was fair play, and he owed her the same kind of honesty. "I thought I would be marrying this time last year. But evidently I couldn't read the character of a person any better than you believe you could. The woman I thought would be my wife, and was about to ask her father for her hand in marriage, was actually seeing someone else at the same time."

"Jake, I'm sorry."

"I've come to realize that perhaps the Lord saved me from myself. The other man had more money and more land, and she wanted a lifestyle of ease now. She didn't want to build that kind of life together. Didn't want to see what the future could be. She wanted it all now."

"Well, I do know one thing. You are much too good for that girl back home."

"Thank you, Julia. I'm not sure of that, but I appreciate you trying to make me feel better." Her words had soothed his heart as nothing else had. And in a way, that made him wonder if time had healed much of his bitterness.

Yet, he wasn't sure he was ready to take a chance on losing his heart again. And even if he were, and if Julia decided to let herself love someone again, she was probably too much a city girl to even think about giving her heart away to a cowboy from Oklahoma.

Most of the women here were probably looking for rich city men, and he'd been down that road before. He loved his life out

West and had big plans for the future, but he still couldn't provide the kind of lifestyle most young women seemed to want now. Although, he had to admit that Julia and the other women at Heaton House didn't seem to have their sights set on finding wealthy men—or any man at all in Julia's case.

Jake found himself wishing things were different and wondered about what could happen if they were . . . and what it would take to make her change her mind.

∞

DINNER THAT NIGHT was a mix of celebrating Jake's sale and a welcome party of sorts for Collin O'Connor, who quickly asked to be called Cole. He seemed as nice as Jake had described, and Julia thought he would fit in with everyone quite nicely. Mrs. Heaton had set him across from Julia and Jake, and everyone else welcomed him into their midst.

"I can't tell you how happy I am to be here. It was quite lonely at times in my other place," Cole said. "But I can tell that will never be a problem here."

"No. You might want to escape these chattering women from time to time," Stephen teased from the other side of Emily, who frowned and nudged him in the arm, "but you will not get lonely."

"I certainly hope not," Mrs. Heaton said. "We do want you to feel at home."

"I already do. So, did Jake tell you what a help he was riding with me yesterday?"

"He told about a scuffle between two men that you broke up. And that you told about stopping a robbery the other day."

"He didn't tell you about his helping me stop one when he rode with me?"

"Jake?" Julia asked. "You didn't mention that."

Jake shrugged and grinned down at her. "I was just along for the ride."

"He roped his man quicker than I did mine."

"You roped a man on the street?" Joe asked. "Good work, man."

"I told the captain about you, and he said to tell you we're always needing good men."

Julia's heart did a kind of twisty flip. Jake could get a job on the mounted police force? And live here? Would he—?

"Just because I can rope doesn't mean I know how to be a police officer."

Of course he wouldn't. What was she thinking? He had a life back in Oklahoma, and he'd be returning to it soon. He had no interest in staying in New York City.

"Many things can be learned about being a policeman. But a good riding and roping man is not easy to find."

"All I'm going to say is that it was one exciting day!" Jake said.

In spite of telling herself that there was no reason to feel let down at his reply and that she knew he wasn't going to accept a job here in the city when he had a ranch to go back to, disappointment settled into Julia's chest. And that told her much more than she wanted to think about.

But she and Jake were just friends. Good ones she hoped. And she was going to have to take extra care to keep from losing her heart to the first man to come close to slipping into it in years.

CHAPTER 10

*T*he next morning Jake stopped in at the meat market and found that Mr. O'Brien had placed an order with Mr. Benson for some of the beef on hand.

"He said he expected to order more in the future," Mr. Benson said. "And my wife said she'd never tasted such good beef, so expect an order from me occasionally. I know I can sell it."

"That's very good news."

"And I'll recommend your beef anytime."

"I thank you, sir."

From there Jake began to set a schedule of sorts for himself for the rest of the week. He'd go out after the boarders left and call on possible accounts before going back to Heaton House for lunch or meeting up with Michael at a nearby cafe. Then he'd spend the afternoon riding before going to escort Julia home. While he enjoyed his rides, he wished Julia could ride more often with him. He was hoping they'd get in a ride on Saturday.

Evenings were filled with playing parlor games after dinner or singing with the others while Julia played the piano or walking to the ice-cream shop. He hadn't had a boring minute since he'd been here, and Jake was beginning to realize that he'd miss being here when he went back home.

Cole talked about being lonely at his old boardinghouse and how happy he was to be at Heaton House, but Jake had only his house to go back to when he went back home. There was no one there to spend his evenings with. Oh, he could visit with his mother and sister and her husband, but he'd still have to go home to an empty house. It'd never bothered him before, but he had a feeling it would now.

And at the moment, he wasn't in any hurry to go back. His mother was enjoying the visit immensely, and his brother-in-law was looking after things back home and was happy Jake was selling their beef, so he certainly wasn't going to rush his mother to return. Although, he probably should.

Lately all he seemed to think about was Julia. What she was doing, making sure he was on time to escort her home, going back and forth between hating that some man had turned her against all men and relief that she was still single. They were friends after all, and nothing more. He should want the best for her. And he did.

The way he bristled when Cole first spoke to her in a flirty manner told Jake he cared more for Julia than was good for him. But he had no right to say anything. And Julia didn't treat the new boarder any differently than she did the others. He knew that she felt her place at Heaton House was to make new boarders feel at home. And she was wonderful at it.

Possibly *too* good, Jake had thought as Cole began to flirt with her. No more than the other men did, but still, it didn't sit well at all with Jake. He'd had most of Julia's attention since he and his mother had come for a visit, and he knew his feelings for her were growing daily, but he didn't know how to stop them from doing so. And he wasn't sure he wanted to any longer.

ON FRIDAY, Julia was just leaving the Barge office when Jake hurried up the walk. Her heartbeat sped up as he asked, "Am I late? My watch must be off."

"No, you're just on time," she assured him. "But I got through early and thought I'd meet you out here. It's so nice out."

"It is that. Can we walk home?"

"Of course. I was hoping you'd want to."

He lightly grasped her arm, and they began to walk in the direction he'd come from. "It was a great day to ride. Are you going to be able to go riding tomorrow?"

Julia's heart fell. She wanted to spend time with him, but she couldn't, not with the excursion to see the Statue of Liberty planned for Sunday afternoon. "I don't think so. My mother called and wanted me to come home tomorrow afternoon. I haven't been to see them in several weeks, and I can't not go."

"Of course not. I understand. But . . . would it be too presumptuous of me to ask to escort you over? I'd love to meet your family."

Her heart did a little flip. "You would?"

"Of course I would. They must be very nice to have a daughter like you. Besides, I haven't been to Brooklyn, and I'd like to see it."

"I'd like for you to. I'll telephone Mama tonight and let her know I'm bringing a friend. But I'll let her know that we are *just* friends. Otherwise she might think differently. I've never brought a man home with me before."

"I feel honored that I'll be the first. Do you think it will be all right with your parents?"

Julia laughed. "I know it will. But if we aren't careful, she'll be plotting to get us together."

"We couldn't have that, could we?" Jake's tone was teasing, but the expression in his eyes had her pulse skittering through her veins.

"I believe you feared your mother might think the same way, didn't you?"

"Well, I've come to understand that we have no control over what our loved ones wish for. But I do understand, and I'll be sure to be on my best behavior."

"You're always on your best behavior."

"Are you saying I'm boring?" Jake grinned down at her.

"You know I'm not. And I hate to miss riding again, but with the plans for Sunday, I had to choose one day or the other."

"I'm glad you chose Saturday. I don't want to visit the Statue of Liberty without you."

Julia told herself not to read anything into his words. They'd talked about visiting the statue the day she'd first shown him around, and she wanted to be there when he saw her.

"I think you'll love it. So how did your day go?"

He told her about his morning, that he'd met Michael for lunch and then gone to ride. "How did your day go?"

"It was good. We had a ship from England, and it went smoothly. No one had to be detained because of illness, and that's rare. There is nearly always someone who must stay in the infirmary for a few days. And no one had to be sent back that I know of."

"I'm glad it all went smoothly."

"So am I."

"Were any of them going out West?"

She chuckled as she remembered telling him about why she'd wanted to go West. "None that I met, but I'm sure there must be a few who are."

"Have you thought anymore about it?"

"Going out West?"

"Yes."

Julia shrugged, almost regretting mentioning it to him. It was doubtful she'd ever go. That was a dream she'd let go of because she was too timid to strike out on her own.

"Probably not. I used to tell myself it was because my family needed me here, but I've recently come to realize that I'm not brave enough to travel by myself."

"I'm sure you'd be fine. You could go back with me and Mother, you know. For a visit, to see how you liked it. You could stay at the boardinghouse. I'm sure you and my sister would get along wonderfully."

That he might want her to visit filled her heart with joy. "Oh Jake, what a nice offer. Still, my mother's health is up and down and I . . . I do love the thought of it, though."

Suddenly Julia realized that she felt more comfortable around Jake Tucker than any man she knew. She'd already shared more with him than anyone, ever. He knew things about her that even her family didn't. How was it she'd come to trust him in the short time he'd been here, when she'd vowed never to trust another man?

"Well, if you change your mind, you'd always be welcome."

His words warmed her heart while the thought of his going back filled her with deep sadness at the same time. "You talk as if you are about to leave. Have you set a date?"

"No, not yet. Mama is having such a good time, and everything is being well taken care of back home. I don't want to rush her."

Julia didn't realize she'd been holding her breath until she released it. She wasn't ready for him to leave—not now and maybe not ever.

But with the open invitation he gave her, her heart filled with hope that even after he left they would remain friends and keep in contact.

As it turned out, Julia's mother wanted them to come for dinner the next evening, so they decided to go for a short ride the next morning.

Jake didn't know who was happier that she'd remembered all the instructions he'd given her—Julia or him. But she seemed quite comfortable as they started out.

"I hope nothing runs across our path today," she said from beside him.

"So do I. But if something does spook Gentle Girl, just remember not to jerk the reins but pull up on them steadily and say stop in a firm tone."

"I'll try."

"You'll do fine. Let's try a different trail. I've found one that has a stream alongside it."

"You lead the way."

"You can stay beside me; the path doesn't narrow as much on this one."

"That's good."

"You seem quite relaxed today."

"It's Gentle Girl. She's such a good horse. I think she likes me."

"Of course she does. You're very likable."

"I am?" She smiled over at him.

Jake's chest tightened as he grinned back. "You are."

"Well, you're very nice, too."

He threw back his head and laughed. "I'm glad you think so."

They turned a bend and then took another turn. "Here's the stream. Isn't it nice here?"

"It's lovely, Jake. Can we stop?"

"Of course." He led the way to the bubbling brook. "Want to get down?"

"I'm not sure I can get back up without a step."

"I'll help you."

"Then yes, I'd like to walk along it for a bit." She pulled up on Gentle Girl's rein and said, "Stop."

Jake was relieved that the horse did what she asked.

Julia smiled at him as he dismounted and went over to help her. His hands spanned her small waist, and she put her hands on his shoulders as he lifted her down. She looked up at him, and the look in her eyes made him hold his breath. The urge to kiss her was swift and strong, but then Gentle Girl turned her head and snickered, and Jake quickly straightened and took his hands away from her waist.

"It's nice here, isn't it?" he asked as they took hold of their horses' reins and walked along the stream.

"It's beautiful. I've been coming to Central Park all my life, but I never knew this was here."

"It was a nice surprise to me. I'm glad you like it. And I'm glad you like horseback riding."

"I do. Thank you for teaching me. I'll never be a great horse-woman, but at least I know how to ride one. It's something I've always wanted to do."

"And I've always wanted to see the Statue of Liberty, and you're going to show it to me tomorrow. Will we be able to go inside it?"

"Yes. We'll take a narrow staircase up to the crown where you can see the city."

"I'm really looking forward to it."

"So am I." Julia sighed and looked at him. "I suppose we should be finishing up our ride, though, so we can freshen up and go see my family. Are you sure you want to do this?"

"Of course I'm sure. Are you changing your mind about—"

"No. But I do have brothers and sisters who can be quite precocious at times."

Jake chuckled. "Thanks for the warning. I'll heed it, and I think I can handle it."

Somehow Julia was sure he could.

Jake helped her to get on Gentle Girl, and they headed for the stables. He was looking forward to meeting her family. He'd like them, he was sure of it.

MARTHA POURED her and Lucy cups of tea after Julia and Jake left for her parents.

Her cousin's eyes were shining as she took the cup from her. "Do you think this means anything, Martha?"

Martha took her seat and shrugged. "I don't know. As far as I know, Julia has never asked a man to meet her parents. And yet, I think they truly like each other as friends."

"But friends can fall in love."

"Of course they can. But I'd think that if things were serious between them, Jake would have told you."

"I would hope that he would have. But you know, young people these days have their own way of doing things, Martha."

"Yes, they do."

"And Jake has seemed happier than I've ever seen him--even when he was courting Caroline. Do you think Julia would move away for someone she loves?"

"I don't know. She used to talk about going out West, but I haven't heard her speak of it in a long while. I think she believes she needs to be here in case her family needs her. Her mother was very ill not long ago and—" she stopped and sighed. "I just don't know what to tell you, Lucy."

"She's a lovely woman, and I like her a lot."

"Yes, so do I. And they would make a beautiful couple. But I don't want to see either of them hurt."

"Neither do I. That's why I haven't questioned Jake about how much time he spends with her or how he feels about her. I've just been praying for the Lord to guide him."

"And I've been doing the same—for him and Julia. And if the Lord needs our help in anyway, I'm sure He'll find a way to let us know."

Lucy nodded. "You are absolutely right. I do hope they have a good time this evening."

"Yes, so do I."

"What do you think of your new boarder?" Lucy asked.

Martha was surprised and quite relieved at her cousin's abrupt change of subject. "Cole? He's a delight, don't you think? I love hearing him talk, and he seems to be fitting in very well."

"Yes, he does. I've seen him looking at Julia quite often. Do you think he's sweet on her?"

Martha sighed on the inside. Evidently it wasn't a change of conversation. She chuckled. "I think he looks at all the female boarders much the same way. He's probably trying to figure out if any of them are taken with one of the men here. They all have such fun together, it's probably hard for a new boarder to figure out who has eyes on whom."

"Yes, I can see how it could be quite confusing. So far the only two I think might feel something they haven't quite come to terms with are my Jake and Julia."

"I agree. And it might be some time before they figure it out."

"That's true. I do so love to have you to talk to about all of this, Martha. I'm beginning to miss Laurie, but when I go home, I'll miss you!"

"I'll miss you and Jake, too. I do wish we lived closer. But perhaps we can visit each other from time to time. I know Gretchen and Maida could take care of things for a week or so, and they'd have Rebecca to call if need be."

"Martha, that would be wonderful. The train ride really isn't so bad, and I'd like to come back again."

"We'll have to plan on it. But for now, I suppose I should go check on our own dinner or Gretchen will be looking for me."

CHAPTER 11

*J*ake enjoyed the trip across the Brooklyn Bridge and the trolley ride to Julia's parents' neighborhood. It wasn't as nice as Gramercy Park, but it was neat and clean. The brownstones lined up quite nicely along the streets as they walked, although they all looked a lot alike.

Julia stopped at one and turned to him. "These brownstones have been around a while and have been made into apartments with each one on a different floor. My parents live on the third floor which isn't good for bringing up groceries, but it has a better view and is more private than the others. It was a good neighborhood to grow up in."

"What made you leave home?"

"It was too crowded. There are seven of us. Four still at home. Two of my brothers left before I did and started families of their own. But we all have tried to help as we could, when Papa lost his job several years ago and when Mama gets sick."

"I'm sorry they've had bad times."

"They are doing better now. Papa got a better job, and Mama seems to have recovered from her last illness. I pray she stays better, but she still seems frail to me at times. The doctor says its asthma. I come and stay overnight and on weekends when I'm needed, but they insist they are fine now."

They headed up the walk, and Julia let herself in the front door. They entered a foyer that was much smaller than his aunt's. She led him up two flights of stairs to the door of her parents' home. She knocked once and then let herself in with her key. "Mama, Papa, we're here," she called.

Then suddenly people seemed to come from every direction. Her parents came first to be followed by four others Jake presumed were her siblings.

"Julia, you came early! That is good," her mother said, giving her eldest daughter a hug and kissing her on the cheek. "I wasn't expecting you for another half hour."

"I thought maybe I could help you with supper," Julia said before making introductions. "Jake, meet my mother and father, Rory and Suzette Olsen." Julia motioned to a woman who looked a lot like her, with red hair and blue eyes and a bright smile much like Julia's, and a man with brown hair and green eyes.

"How do you do, Mr. And Mrs. Olsen?"

"Mama, Papa, this is Jake Tucker. He's related to Mrs. Heaton, and he and his mother are here for a visit."

Her father held out his hand, and Jake took it. It was strong and calloused. He seemed to be sizing Jake up, and then he nodded and smiled. "It's nice to meet you, Mr. Tucker. How are you liking the city?"

"I do like it, sir. But I'm from Oklahoma, and it's a bit less crowded there."

Julia's father chuckled and nodded. "I understand."

Jake turned to Julia's mother. "It's very nice to meet you, Mrs. Tucker. I can see that Julia takes after you."

"Oh, she's much prettier than I am," Julia's mother said.

"Suzette, she looks just like you did at her age. I remember, you know," Mr. Olsen said.

A look passed between the couple, and Jake had a feeling they were still as much in love as they'd been from the beginning, only maybe more so.

Then Julia introduced him to her brothers and sisters ranging in age from around ten to fifteen or sixteen, and they surrounded him and began to ask all kinds of questions about Oklahoma and the West.

"Children, quiet a moment," Mrs. Olsen said. "Papa, why don't you take Mr. Tucker to the parlor while Julia and I finish up dinner?"

Jake felt an instant of uncertainty as Julia flashed him a smile and a look that reminded him that he'd said he could handle her siblings. Now was the time. He smiled back and would have winked at her had her family not been surrounding them.

"Yes, that is a good idea, Mama," Mr. Olsen said. "Come this way, Mr. Tucker. Children, you may come, too, if you promise to behave."

"Leila and Carleen can come and help Julia and me," Mrs. Tucker said.

"Mama!" both girls said at the same time.

"Girls, now," Mrs. Olsen said in a soft but firm voice. "You'll get a chance to get to know Mr. Tucker at dinner."

"Yes, Mama," the oldest, Leila, said.

Julia smiled at Jake as the boys led him away and then followed her mother into the kitchen. The apartment wasn't very large, and Jake could see how Julia felt she must get out on her own if for no other reason than to give the others more space. But it was neat and clean and cozy.

Mr. Olsen motioned for him to take a seat in the chair adjacent to the one he took.

The boys, Keegan and Ryan, took seats on the floor in front of them.

"Now, Mr. Tucker, I know the boys are full of questions about Oklahoma and out West, because Julia has told us you are a rancher out there. But what I want to know is how you got our daughter to bring you to meet us?"

"She's become a good friend to me, and I just asked her if I could come along. And please call me Jake, sir."

Mr. Olsen chuckled and nodded. "And that's all it took—just asking?"

"Yes sir, it is."

"Well, I'm glad she did. Now boys, you may ask your questions."

"What's it like out there where you live?" Keegan asked. "Are there gunfights every day?"

"Not where I live."

"Do you ride horses every day?" Ryan asked.

"I do."

"And we heard there are Indians out West. What is that like?" Keegan asked.

Jake chuckled and finally relaxed. He loved talking about Oklahoma and the life out there, and these two boys reminded him of his cousins boys back home. He would love to show them around. But maybe he could help them see it as he did. He launched into a detailed description of what his ranch was like.

JULIA HELPED her mother in the kitchen, trying to listen to what was going on in the parlor, but it was impossible. Her sisters were full of questions, and there was no evading them.

"Is he courting you, Julia?" twelve-year-old Carleen asked.

"No, he's not."

"But you've never brought a man home before," Carleen said.

"He's very handsome, Julia," fifteen-year-old Leila said. "Do you like him a lot?"

"Yes, I do, but we're just good friends, Leila."

"Go on with ya. I saw the way you looked at him."

"I look at all my friends the same way, Leila." Or did she? She did have special feelings for Jake. He was the first really good male friend she'd ever had. Her sister must be reading things into the way she looked at Jake.

"I doubt that," her sister said.

"How would you know?"

"I've seen girls look at their beaus the very same way. You just don't want to admit you care about him."

"Like you look at Chad?" Carleen asked."

"I do not look at him in the same way!" Leila said.

"Chad? And who is he?" Julia asked, smiling that she could turn the tables on her sister.

"A new family moved in downstairs, and their son is the same age as Leila," Julia's mother said. "They've become friends. He's a nice boy."

"And how does she look at Chad, Carleen?" Julia asked, grinning at Leila.

"Like you look at Mr. Tucker! You'd have to see it, I guess."

"I don't look at Chad any way in particular, Carleen!"

"Girls! Why don't you go set the table? The rolls will be out of the oven soon, and we'll be eating."

Julia's sisters hurried out of the room, with Carleen still denying she had special feelings for the boy downstairs.

"Thank you, Mama. That conversation was—"

"Too close for comfort? You do like this man a lot, don't you, daughter?"

"I've never had a good male friend before, Mama. I'm enjoying it, but that's all we are."

"Are you sure? I not only saw how you looked at him, I saw how he looked at *you*."

Julia shook her head. She was afraid of this. Mama wanted a match. "And how was that?"

"Like your papa looked at me when he asked to court me."

Julia held her breath and then released it. If only. "Mama, Jake has a ranch back in Oklahoma he'll be going back to soon. There's no sense thinking that we are more than friends. Besides, this is my home. I wouldn't leave you and Papa, not with your health so fragile and—"

"My health is fine, Julia. The doctor said so. Papa and I don't want you thinking you can't have a life because of us. Things are much better now. He has a good job, and I am feeling well. It's time you quit worrying about us and got on with your life."

"But Mama—"

"No more talk now, it's time to eat. Grab the stew and I'll bring the bread."

Julia grabbed the potholders and picked up the tureen of stew while her mother popped the rolls into a basket. They put the dishes on the table, and her mother sent Leila back for the pitcher of water and Carleen for the butter, while she called the men to dinner.

Julia looked at Jake as he entered the room, but he seemed in good spirits, and she could tell he'd won her brothers over. Even her father seemed taken by him. Well, why not? Even after warning herself against him from the first moment she'd looked up into his eyes, he'd won her over. Hadn't he?

❦

"You come back anytime, Jake," Mr. Olsen said as he and Julia said their goodbyes.

"Thank you, sir. I'd love to—if I can get your daughter to bring me." Jake turned to her mother. "Your stew was delicious, Mrs. Olsen. And your rolls were light as air."

"Why, thank you, Jake. Like Papa says, you come by anytime. And you don't even have to have Julia with you."

"Thank you, ma'am."

"'Night, Mama and Papa," Julia said as she gave a little tug to his arm. "I'll talk to you soon."

"You'd better," her mother said. "Goodnight."

Julia eased them out the door and down the stairs. "I thought I'd never get you out of there."

"Why, Julia, I really like your family. I had a lot of fun tonight, and I thought I was on my best behavior. Did I do something wrong?"

"No! They all love you, but that's the problem. Mama is going to start asking me if you've asked to court me. And if not her, then the girls will, and—"

"Would that be so bad?" Now why had he said that? What was he thinking?

"Jake, don't be silly. I don't want Mama getting her hopes up. You have no intention of asking to court me, and you'll be going back to Oklahoma soon."

That part was true. He couldn't argue with it. But he could wish things were different. Still, he didn't want her to be upset with him. "I'm sorry, Julia."

"You've done nothing wrong, Jake. But you feel the same way about your mother, don't you? You don't want to give her reason to believe—"

Jake held up his hands. "You're right. I understand. But my mother hasn't said anything about you . . ." He paused. "And that's just strange, considering that we are together a lot. That's not like her at all."

"Well, she's been having a nice visit with Mrs. Heaton, and it probably hasn't crossed her mind that you might get interested in anyone here. She knows you'll be going back home. On the other hand, *my* mother is probably talking Papa's ear off with all the possibilities she's dreaming of."

Jake laughed. "Oh Julia, I doubt it. And you'll set her straight if she is."

"Yes, I'm sure I will have to. But I'm glad they liked you and that you had a good time."

"So am I." He had enjoyed meeting her family, and he wouldn't mind visiting again. But he didn't think this was the time to bring that up.

They took a hack across the bridge and back to Heaton House. It was worth the money to have the time with Julia.

On the way back, she pointed out first one building then another, and he entertained her with all the questions her brothers asked him about horses and ranching and what it was like riding a train. "It was near non-stop while you were helping your mother with supper."

"I'm sure it was. They usually take over a conversation anytime they can."

They got back to Heaton House just as everyone was leaving the parlor.

"Well, I guess it's goodnight," he said as they paused in the foyer. "Again, thank you for taking me to see your family."

"Thank you for escorting me there and back."

"You're welcome. See you in the morning."

Julia nodded and headed upstairs while Jake went down to his room. It wasn't until then that Jake realized Julia had never answered his question about whether his asking to court her would be a bad thing. But neither did she sound happy about having to explain things to her mother. Although, she seemed genuinely glad they all liked each other. What did any of that mean?

How he wished he could understand women! Especially this one!

AFTER CHURCH THE NEXT DAY, everyone was in high spirits on the way to Bedloe's Island where the Statue of Liberty stood. It was a beautiful day, the light breeze on the water making it feel a little cooler than it really was. Michael had bought ferry tickets for everyone, and Mrs. Heaton had prepared a picnic lunch to eat on the island.

Julia stood beside Jake as the ferry headed toward the statue.

"This is nice," Jake said. "I've never ridden a ferry before. And seeing New York and New Jersey at the same time is quite a sight. There are a *lot* of people living up here."

Julia chuckled. "That's an understatement."

"Yes, it is. Do you ever feel closed in?"

Julia shook her head. "Not really, but I was raised here. It has grown in that time, but the biggest change is how tall the buildings are getting to be. I don't really know anything else."

"And yet you wanted to go out West? Why was that?"

"I think I just wanted an adventure. It seemed exciting to think about building a life for one's self in a new place. But—" Julia broke off and shrugged. "I would like to see other parts of the country one day, but truthfully, as independent as I think I am, it would be difficult to take off on my own." She couldn't believe she'd confided in Jake about that. She'd never said so much to anyone. What was it about this man that had her telling him things she'd never told anyone else? "Anyway, I may never leave here, and I've decided that perhaps I should be glad that I live where I do."

"I can understand why a woman wouldn't feel easy about traveling so far alone. But maybe if she knew the people she'd be going to see it wouldn't be so bad. I'd love to show you Oklahoma."

Her heart fluttered at his suggestion. She had been thinking that maybe she could go visit—not plan on staying, but for a visit with Jake and his family ever since he'd brought it up the other day. "Thank you for suggesting that, Jake. A visit does sound nice."

They both propped their arms on the railing as they neared Bedloe's Island. Julia pointed out Ellis Island where they were building the new immigration buildings. "It won't be long now before we move back over there. I'll get to ride the ferry to work every day again."

"I hadn't thought of that, but I suppose that's how you'd have to get over there."

The ferry made a turn, and the Statue of Liberty shined brightly in the sunlight.

After looking at the landmark, Jake turned to Julia. "You know, she is pretty, but she doesn't hold a candle to you. You always look very nice, but you look especially nice today."

Julia could feel color flood her face. She'd worn a new outfit today, one she'd hired Betsy to make for her. It was a pale pink and green floral with white lace over the bodice. She was wearing a wide brimmed white hat with a pale pink lining and white roses decorating it. She felt quite feminine and summery in it. "Thank you. Betsy made it for me."

"She's quite talented, isn't she?"

"She is. She stays quite busy, too. Making Georgia's wedding dress and trousseau garnered her several new clients. I fear she won't have time to sew for us much longer."

"I imagine she'll make time."

"I hope so."

"Thank you again for taking me to meet your family. They are very nice. I've been chuckling over some of the things your brothers said all morning."

Julia had been trying to put off thinking about the evening before when he'd asked her if it would be a bad thing if he asked to court her all morning—especially after she'd dreamed that he had, and she'd said yes!

She couldn't begin dreaming impossible dreams. But she had a feeling that his invitation to come for a visit would make it impossible to stop them.

The ferry docked, and she and Jake joined Michael and Violet, Mrs. Heaton and his mother, and the others as they all disembarked with several baskets of food and blankets for their picnic and stood on solid ground once more.

"I'm glad we left right after church. I think we might have beaten the crowd," Mrs. Heaton said. "Shall we find a spot to have our lunch before you climb to the crown or after?"

"Let's eat now, Mother," Rebecca suggested. "The little ones will be getting cranky if they get hungry."

"Then let's find a spot."

They all looked around, and it was Jake who found the perfect spot under two trees. In only a few moments, the blankets were spread while Julia and the other women helped put out the food. When everything was set up, they all began to help themselves to the spread.

Once she'd fixed her plate, Julia looked around for a spot to sit.

"Over there," Betsy said. "Jake is trying to get your attention."

Julia looked in the direction she was pointing, and sure enough, Jake began to motion for them to come over to where he was, along with Cole.

Betsy looked at Julia. "Come on, Julia, I'd kind of like to get to know Cole a little better . . . And Jake doesn't want to sit beside anyone but you."

"That's not true," Julia said as they headed toward the two men.

"It *is* true. Julia, he *never* sits beside anyone else, and you know it."

She hadn't thought about it before, but now that Betsy had mentioned it, she realized her friend was right. And she had to admit that it pleased her that Jake had saved her a spot beside him today.

But she was surprised that the group hadn't given them a hard time about it—except perhaps that they realized Jake would be leaving to go back home before long. Something she kept telling herself. But she didn't want to think about it today. She wanted to enjoy the day.

Jake held out a hand to steady her while she sank down beside him. Michael stood and offered the blessing before they ate, and Julia added to it silently, praying that Jake enjoyed the outing and that she kept her heart whole while enjoying every minute she could with him. She knew the Lord would get her through the pain of seeing him go, but she just wasn't going to think about his leaving today.

❀

"MY, THAT WAS A CLIMB," Jake said as they reached the Statue of Liberty's crown.

"It was, but the view is quiet worth it, as you'll see," Julia assured him. She led him over to the first window, and Jake had to admit she was right. It was beautiful up here. He looked down and could see his mother and aunt sitting in the shade, watching the children.

"I though Georgia and Sir Tyler might join us today. Do you know why they couldn't come?" he asked.

"Her parents are arriving today. They're going to have us all over for dinner one night while they are here, though."

"That's nice. I'd like to see them again, and I know mother would, too," Jake said as they walked to the next window.

"I think they may have to go back to England soon, though. They've had word that Sir Tyler's father hasn't been well."

"I'm sorry to hear that. I'll pray he gets better."

Julia smiled, and he thought once more how pretty she looked today. Her beautiful red hair stood out under the brim of her white hat and the white lace of her dress. She looked almost like a bride and. . . What was he thinking? She'd told him he was being silly when he'd asked if wanting to court her would be so bad.

But he hadn't felt silly when he asked the question. He'd really wanted to know the answer.

She'd said it was because he was leaving and then today said it would be hard to make a trip alone. Then she'd seemed open to perhaps visiting one day. Jake sighed inwardly. Did this woman have any idea how she confused him?

They moved around to another window. "Look, you can see both states at one time," Julia said.

"It is quite a sight. I can't believe how big this statue is." He turned to Julia. "I wanted to get a photo but I forgot my camera."

"Don't worry, Millicent always has hers. I'll go ask her if she'll take a photograph for you."

Julia hurried off to speak to one of the former boarders and her husband who'd joined them. Then all three came hurrying over to him.

"I'd love to take some photos for you, Jake," Millicent said. "Just stand there, and I'll try to get some good shots of you and the view out the window. Julia, you stand beside him."

"I don't need to be in the photo. You won't see near as much of the view."

"I'll take some both ways. Now you stand beside him and I'll snap. Then you can move away and I'll get just Jake."

"Please, Julia," Jake said in a low voice that only she could hear. "I'd like a photo of you to take home with me."

How could she refuse a request like that? She wouldn't mind having one of him for after he left, either. She'd have to ask Millicent to make her a copy, too.

Julia nodded her agreement, and the two of them posed several times for Millicent, who coached them on where to look and how to turn so she could get the best shots. She had them moving from window to window.

"I think that's enough for now, Millicent," Julia said.

"One more. For this one, simply look at each other and smile."

Without even thinking, they did as she asked.

"Ok, now you can move away, Julia, and I'll get a couple of Jake alone. Then some more in front of the Lady when we go back down."

"Thank you, Millicent. I'll be glad to pay for the film and the developing."

"You're welcome, and I'll get them to you soon."

Julia and Jake headed back down the steep winding staircase.

"It's quite a climb, but as you said, it was worth it," Jake said. "Although the view was of cities, up so high there were wide open skies like back home."

"So if you lived in the crown you would feel right at home?" Julia asked.

Jake laughed. "No, but it was nice to be up so high."

"You need to talk to Millicent's husband, Matt. He's a builder and worked on the tallest building in the city. He loves the view from up high."

"Sounds very interesting."

Once they were out in the sunshine again, Jake suggested walking around the small island while they waited for everyone else to get through touring the statue. It didn't take long, and by the time they reached the front of the statue again, everyone was getting ready to board the ferry once more.

"Hurry, you two. I want to get that photo," Millicent said.

Jake grabbed Julia's hand and they ran to the base of the statue while Millicent got as far away as she could to get all she could of them and the statue.

"Smile!" Millicent was known for wanting her subjects to look happy or at least natural, instead of the solemn looks so many photographs depicted.

They did as ordered, and then Jake chuckled. "She's quite demanding, isn't she?"

Julia giggled. "She always manages to get wonderful shots, so I don't question her."

"I look forward to seeing them."

"All right everyone," Michael said, "we'd better board or we'll be spending the night here."

"Well, nice as it is, I don't think I want to do that," Jake said. He and the men grabbed up the baskets and folded blankets and they all hurried to the waiting ferry.

Julia could see the satisfied expressions on everyone's faces. It'd been a good day, and she was glad she'd been part of it for Jake. He'd have good memories to take home. And—Julia tried to ignore the little twist of pain near her heart that the thought gave her—she'd have good memories to keep here.

CHAPTER 12

$\mathcal{W}$ith Independence Day nearly upon them, temperatures seemed to climb daily during the next week. Everyone was complaining of the heat—even Jake who was used to hot temperatures out West.

He had been successful in finding two more clients for Oklahoma beef, and after speaking to Mr. Benson at the meat market, he felt he'd establish a good business relationship with the man.

"I handed out a roast or two to the owners of a couple more restaurants and they've asked me to continue to carry your beef. So, I'd like to add an order over and above what I'll carry for your other customers."

"Thank you, Mr. Benson. I'm happy to supply you all the beef you can sell," Jake said. He hadn't expected these kinds of results quite so fast.

As he left the meat market on Friday, he was more than happy with the business he'd managed to acquire for Oklahoma ranchers during the past few weeks. His brother-in-law was very excited, and so were the members of the Cattlemen's Association, judging from the telegraphs he'd received in short order. It'd certainly do for now. And he could always come back to try to get more business.

That was a thought he'd not run by anyone, but he knew that he'd be back whether on Association business or his own. And he knew that he should be thinking about going back home— talking to his mother about when she might be ready. But much as he longed for more open skies and the Oklahoma sunrises and sunsets, he wasn't quite ready to leave yet.

He felt torn, and he knew he could no longer deny that it was because of his growing feelings for Julia. He didn't want to leave her. And when he'd asked her if it'd be so bad if he did ask to court her, he'd suddenly realized that was exactly what he wanted to do.

And yet, he had no reason to think she wanted him to stay. And even if she did, her friendship meant so much to him he didn't want to chance ruining it or losing it.

Dear Lord, please help me here. I know now that I only thought I loved Caroline. But I believe what I loved was the idea of having a wife and family of my own, but Caroline wasn't right for me and I know it now. Thank You for saving me from making a mistake.

As for Julia, I don't want a broken heart again, for this time it would be worse. But I trust that You will help me through it, should that happen. Please help me to know if Julia and I are meant to be together and what to do about it either way. In Jesus' name I pray, amen.

There, he'd admitted how he felt and asked for help. For now, there was nothing more to do except enjoy her company as much as he could before it was time to leave. And at least he knew it wouldn't be until after Independence Day. His mother was looking forward to celebrating the holiday in the city. With that realization, his heart felt lighter as he headed toward the Barge office to escort Julia home.

She looked excited when he arrived, and they'd no more than started up the walk than she turned to him. "Jake, I don't have to work on the Fourth! My supervisor let me off, so I'll get to be in on all the festivities with you all."

Now that made him happy. "That is wonderful, Julia."

"Yes, it is. With you and your mother here, I was hoping to be off, but it's never a sure thing. But Mrs. Johnson told me she'd fill in if needed. So, that's my news—how did your day go?"

"Very well. Mr. Benson wants to carry our beef on a regular basis and already has customers of his own asking for it."

"That's even better than my news."

"Not to me. Watching parades and having a picnic wouldn't be the same without you." He watched as a delicate color spread up to her cheeks and hoped that meant she felt the same way.

"You'd have enjoyed it. The boarders would have seen to it. And I would be back in time to watch the fireworks from wherever we go to see them. But I'm glad I'll be able to enjoy it all with you."

He didn't dare want to read too much into her words, but a flame of hope flared, and he didn't want to tamp it down.

They arrived at Heaton House just in time to freshen up and joined the others just as his aunt called them all to dinner.

With the holiday weekend on them, everyone was ready to begin the festivities.

"Gretchen made ice-cream for later," Aunt Martha said. "That should help to cool us all down."

"And we don't have to walk in the heat to get it," Betsy said. "I do hope the weather cools down a bit before Independence Day."

"Why don't we all go swimming tomorrow?" Joe suggested. "I'd suggest waiting until the Fourth, but with parades, picnics, and fireworks, I'm not sure we can work it all in."

"Sounds good to me," Jake said. "But I didn't bring any swimming clothes with me."

"You can get something at Macy's," Emily suggested.

"Or at Siegel-Cooper," Stephen added.

"I've got an extra swimsuit you can use," Joe said. "Or you can rent one at the beach. It'd be silly for you to buy one when you'll be going home soon."

Julia's heart twisted at the very thought of Jake leaving soon but she tried to ignore the pain and act excited about the outing. "It does sound good," Julia said. "What do you think? Should we plan for it?"

"Let's do!" Betsy said.

"Just remember not to get too worn out," Mrs. Heaton said. "We're all invited over to the Walkers' house tomorrow evening. Georgia's parents are here."

"That's right. Well, let's go mid-morning and come back early," Julia said.

"Anytime is good with me," Jake said.

"We can take the trolley to catch a steamship to Coney Island. It'll be the fastest way since we have to be back early," Joe said.

Jake was glad they'd be here for the holiday. He wasn't even going to think of leaving until afterward. His mother seemed in no hurry, and things were going well according to his last telegram from his brother-in-law. He'd think about going before too long. Maybe next week, but not now.

THEY'D TELEPHONED the old boarders and invited them to go, too, but only Millicent and Matt could accept the invitation. They arrived right after breakfast and joined the boarders who could go as they all set out for the beach. Emily had to work, but Stephen had managed to get the day off.

"I almost feel guilty for being able to go while Emily has to work, but I'm not sure why," he said. "We don't even work for the same company. Wish she worked for us. I'd have tried to give her the day off."

"She understood. At least she'll be off tomorrow and Monday," Julia said, wondering if there was anything going on between those two. They worked for competing stores and teased each other about which one was best on a regular basis. Stephen kept trying to get her to quit Macy's and come to work for Siegel-Cooper, but Emily said she was happy where she was. They seemed to have a friendly rivalry, but Julia had never thought of them as a possible couple until now.

As they caught the trolley, everyone seemed in a holiday mood, and Julia was as excited as everyone else. It would be a wonderful way to start the weekend. She hadn't been swimming in a long time.

She had a feeling the Tuckers would be going back to Oklahoma before long, although Jake hadn't said much about it. But they'd been there longer than she'd thought they would be, and she knew the visit had to come to an end at some point.

Julia tried to ignore the pang in her heart at the thought of Jake leaving. But it was a reality she was going to have to accept. Life wouldn't be the same without him around to ask about her day or to escort her home from work. Perhaps she should have discouraged that and made excuses for not spending so much time with him.

But no—the truth was she wouldn't do it any differently if she could. She'd enjoyed every minute of each day she'd spent with him, and hard as it would be to see him leave, she'd have good memories to treasure.

But somehow that thought didn't give her comfort as they traveled by trolley to the steamship port that would take them to Coney Island.

"You're awfully quiet today," Jake said, bringing her out of her thoughts.

"I was just thinking how nice it'll be to go swimming. It's been a long time. Hope I haven't forgotten how."

"You'll remember, and I'll be there to save you if you get into trouble. I wouldn't let anything happen to you, you should know that."

Her heart slammed against her chest at the expression in his eyes. Jake cared about her, too. She knew that. Their friendship could continue even from a distance. At least until he found someone to marry. But he'd said he wasn't interested in finding a mate, so perhaps—

Julia broke off the thought. She didn't know what the future held, but she did know that they were friends for now, and she was going to enjoy it while she could. "Jake, would you. . .have you, ever kept up a friendship by corresponding through letters?

"I've never had the need to before now. And yes, I would definitely be willing to keep up a friendship that way if it was with you.

"Well, I know you'll be leaving one of these days, and I—I'd like our friendship to continue."

"So would I, Julia. I've been trying to think of how to ask you the same thing, so thank you for doing it for me."

"Well, good. Now we have that out of the way, we don't have to worry about it."

"And it turns out that we didn't need to worry anyway." Jake grinned down at her.

The trolley arrived at the port, and they all hurried onto the steamship. Everyone gathered at the railing and filled the twenty minutes it took to get to Coney Island with conversation.

When they landed, they hurried to the bathhouses to change and put their things in the lockers they rented.

Julia, Millicent, and Betsy changed into their swimsuits. Julia's was not new, but no more than she'd used it, it looked fine.

All their suits were all much the same with three-quarters-length wool bloomers and a sleeveless wool over-dress that was belted. Everything was worn over black stockings and laced slippers. Only the colors were different. Julia's was navy and white, Betsy's was red and white, and Millicent's was striped blue and red. Betsy had a swim cap on, but Julia and Millicent had braided their hair, and now they took the pins holding it up out and let their braids hang down their backs.

"I've never been able to keep those caps on," Julia said.

"No, neither have I," Millicent said. "I think they are a pain to keep up with."

"You just don't tie them tight enough." Betsy went on to show them how she did.

When they were ready, they hurried outside to find the men all in one-piece suits that appeared much easier to get on. But modesty made the girls look away and pretend they didn't notice the muscled arms they'd only imagined through shirts before.

Julia felt her face flush and quickly said, "Let's find a spot before it gets too crowded."

They all headed to an empty spot near the water.

"I'm glad we got here when we did. It's already getting crowded," Stephen said.

Jake spread out one of the blankets Mrs. Heaton had provided for them and looked out to sea.

The waves were ebbing and flowing, inviting them to come play.

"Is it cold, do you think?" he asked.

"Yes," Julia said. "At least at first it is. We'll get used to it, though."

They all headed out to the waves and braved the cold water, splashing each other and laughing.

"We have to go deeper to get all wet, then it won't feel so cold," Julia said. They walked out until the water was deep enough to swim and gasped as they inched into the sea.

For the next hour, they let the waves take them out and push them back in, swimming with the flow and not against it.

When they came ashore to dry off, they were all shivering until the sun had a chance to warm them once more. The girls began making a sand castle while the men swam near the shore.

When it began to feel hot, Julia decided to go back in. She lay on her back and floated until she heard Betsy yelling from the shore, "Julia, turn back! You're going out to far!"

Julia turned over and treaded water to see that she had indeed drifted a bit further than she was comfortable with so she began to swim back to shore.

She was a good swimmer, but she suddenly got caught up in seaweed that didn't want to let go. She went underwater to try to release her ankle and pulled most of the seaweed away. Then she burst up to take a deep breath before going back under to pull the rest off.

She thought she heard yelling from the shore but couldn't make out what they were saying as she began to swim back. She was captured by another batch of seaweed and took a deep breath and held it as she went back under.

❀

At Betsy's words, Jake turned just in time to see Julia go under water. "Is she a strong swimmer?"

"I don't know."

Jake dove in and began to swim. *Dear Lord, please let her be all right! Please let me get to her in time!*

She went under again. When she came back up, she only swam a couple of arm's lengths before she went down again. *Oh Lord, please don't let me lose her. Not now that I—* He reached her and pulled her up. She swallowed and began to choke.

"Don't die on me, Julia! Don't you dare die on me. Not now. Not when—"

"Jake!" She coughed. "What are you doing? Let go of me!"

Jake looked at her as she pulled out of his arms, and they both began to tread water. "Julia? We thought you were drowning! You went down three times before I got to you!"

"I kept getting caught in seaweed, and I was trying to get out of it."

"Do you have any idea how frightened we were?" Panicked was more like it. He'd never been so scared in his life.

"No, and I'm sorry you were worried. But as you can see, I'm all right."

"And I'm thankful that you are."

They began to swim toward shore where the rest of the boarders waited.

"Julia! You're all right! We thought you were drowning!"

"I know and I'm sorry." She went on to explain what had happened, while Jake watched. He truly thought he might lose her before he'd had a chance to let her know how much he cared about her. And even he hadn't realized how much that was until now. The fact was he loved this woman, and he didn't even want to imagine what life might be like without her.

"Next time don't float out so far," Betsy said.

"I'll be more watchful, I promise."

"Well, I'm just glad you weren't drowning like we thought."

"So am I."

"Well, after all this, we probably should be getting back. Remember, we have a party to go to this evening," Millicent suggested.

"Yes, I think we've had enough sun for one day," Betsy said.

"I know we've had enough excitement for today," Stephen said.

He didn't know the half of it. Jake's heart was still pounding at the realization that he'd admitted to himself that he loved Julia. But what was he going to do about it?

They gathered up their things, went to change, and caught the next ferry to take them to the pier. Everyone was tired from the sun and fun, if it could be called that after the scare Julia gave them. Once they got to dry land and on their trolley, Joe and Stephen catnapped while Millicent and Betsy chattered about what they were going to wear that night.

Julia seemed quieter than usual, but when Jake looked over at her, she smiled. "Thank you for coming to save me, Jake. No one has ever done anything nicer for me."

"Any time," he said in a voice that sounded deeper than usual, even to him. But he meant what he'd said. He'd do anything to keep her safe. But how was he going to do it from Oklahoma?

They arrived home in plenty of time to freshen up and get dressed for the party next door, but the girls hurried upstairs as if they only had minutes to spare.

Jake was grinning as he headed down the hall.

"Oh Jake, I'm glad you're back!" his mother said as she came out of the study. She sounded quite excited.

"What's happened?"

"Come into Martha's study so I can tell you. She just went to the kitchen to brew us a pot of tea to celebrate."

"Celebrate what, Mother?"

"She held out the piece of paper in her hand. "I've read this three times now, and I still can't believe it."

"Mother, what are you talking about?"

"I received this letter from Laurie today and . . . you're going to become an uncle come January."

"What?" Jake began to grin. "And you'll be a grandmother!"

"Yes, I will. We must think about leaving soon. I want to be there to help her with the boardinghouse so she doesn't overdo and . . ."

There it was. Jake didn't even hear what his mother said next. He knew they'd be leaving, but now she was ready to go and he wasn't. How could he leave now when he'd just realized he was in love with Julia? All he could think about was how to find out if she could ever feel the same way about him.

CHAPTER 13

*J*ulia wondered if she'd heard Jake right. Had he really told her not to die when he was pulling her up from the water? He'd sounded frantic and frightened and . . . he cared for her. She could hear it in his voice, see it in his eyes.

That still didn't mean he felt more than friendship for her. Had she thought he was going to drown, she might have said the same thing. Only Julia knew her feelings had grown way past friendship. Oh, if that was all she could ever have with him, she'd take it, but she longed for more and could no longer deny it—especially not to herself.

But how did she keep everyone else from knowing how she felt? He'd be going back home one of these days, and she didn't want to endure her friend's pitying looks.

Could she let him back home go without letting him know how she felt? Should she tell him? *Dear Lord, I don't know what to do. Please help me.*

She'd washed her hair to get the salt water out of it and put it up into a chignon. And since Jake had liked the dress she'd worn on the outing last Sunday, she put it on again. It was a Sunday best so should be fine for Georgia's dinner party.

She joined the others in the parlor just as Jake came up from downstairs. He looked very handsome in his Western dress clothes. His shoulders seemed even broader than usual, and after today, she knew firsthand how strong his arms were. And how safe she'd felt in them.

He smiled across the room and headed in her direction.

"Looks like you got a little too much sun today—probably from all that floating you did."

"I believe I did overdo it a bit." She smiled and shook her head. "Not ladylike at all."

"You are one of the most ladylike women I know, sunburn and all."

"And *you* are full of blarney tonight." She grinned up at him.

He looked her in the eye. "No, I'm telling the truth."

If her face could get any redder, Julia was sure it did now. Something seemed different about Jake tonight, but she didn't know exactly what it was.

"Are we all ready?" Mrs. Heaton asked.

"I believe we are all here and accounted for," Stephen said.

"Then let's be on our way."

It was a merry group that headed next door. Emily and Cole had made it home from work, and they wanted to know all about the Coney Island excursion.

"Have we got a story to tell you! But it's too long to begin now," Betsy said as they marched up the steps to the front door.

Mr. Tate, Sir Tyler's butler, welcomed them all inside and led them to a parlor twice the size of Mrs. Heaton's.

Georgia and Sir Tyler came forward to greet them and introduce Georgia's parents to those who hadn't met them yet.

Julia smiled as Mr. and Mrs. Marshall greeted Jake and his mother.

The two women shared a hug as Mrs. Marshall said, "I am just so glad we timed our visit with yours, Lucy! I never expected to see you here."

"So am I," Jake's mother said. "And I'm so glad you came when you did. Jake and I will be leaving soon to go home, and I would have hated to hear that I'd missed you."

Julia's heart sank as she glanced over at Jake to find his gaze on her. His eyes looked as troubled as she felt, and she wondered what he was thinking and if they'd decided on a date to leave. But she quickly broke eye contact so that he wouldn't be able to see how upset she was at the news.

"And I have more news to share," his mother continued. "I just received a letter from Laurie and found out that I'm to become a grandmother come the first of the year!"

"Lucy, that is wonderful news," Mrs. Marshall said. "I'm so happy for you, and I can understand why you are excited to be going home."

Julia could understand, too, but it was all she could do not to run out of the room. *Dear Lord, please don't let me cry. Please help me to get through this evening without ruining it for everyone else.*

She was more than thankful when Mr. Tate came back into the room just then to announce that dinner was ready. There were place cards, and she was relieved to see that she was seated on the opposite end of the table from Jake. She didn't even know what to say to him, and she wasn't sure she could bear hearing about their plans to leave.

Dear Lord, please help me. I don't know how to handle all of this. Please give me guidance.

"Julia, what a surprise to be seated by you," Cole said. "How did your beach outing go today?'

"Wait until we tell you," Betsy said from the other side of him. "She floated out too far, and I shouted for her to come back. Then she went under, and Jake swam out to save her."

"We watched as she went under two more times before he got to her, and we all thought she was drowning," Stephen said from across the table.

Julia decided to step into the conversation so that it didn't get too out of hand. "But as it turned out, I wasn't in danger of drowning after all. I'd gotten caught up in some seaweed and was just trying to free myself."

She couldn't keep from glancing down the table at Jake. His gaze was on her, his expression somber. What was he thinking? He had tried to save her life, and she would never, ever forget it. "Still, I'll always be thankful that I have friends who care enough to try to save me from myself."

She was rewarded with the hint of a smile just before his attention was drawn away by someone on the other end of the table. Relieved as she'd been that she hadn't been seated beside him, now she missed the chance to be near him.

Whatever was she going to do when he went back to Oklahoma? She blinked against the tears building behind her eyes. *Dear Lord, please get me through tonight and help me to think this all through so that I don't give away how I truly feel,* she prayed once more.

"Well, I'm certainly glad that you are here to tell the whole story," Cole said, drawing her attention.

"Thank you. So am I." To try to get her mind off Jake and the fact that he'd soon be leaving, Julia began to converse with the new boarder. "How was your day, Cole? Will you have to work over Independence Day?"

"It was not a bad day, although I'd much rather have been at the beach with you all. And yes, I do have to work on the holiday, but I'll be off in time to see the fireworks."

"That's the best part, but it's too bad you won't be able to picnic with us," Betsy said.

Julia had a feeling that her friend was trying to draw Cole's attention and she couldn't blame her. He was a good-looking man, and Betsy's heart was whole. Julia needed to leave her to it. She gave her attention to the meal as Cole was drawn into Betsy's conversation. Then she tried not to listen too hard to the conversation going on at the other end of the table to see if any mention was made of when the Tuckers would be leaving.

She was quite relieved when dinner was over and they all gathered back in the parlor. And she was more than thankful when Mrs. Heaton came over to her and asked, "You don't look like you feel well, Julia. Did you get too much sun today?"

Thank You, Lord, for giving me a way out of this predicament. She could get out of here. "I believe I got too much of it all—sun, surf and sea. Do you think I might be able to slip next door without hurting Georgia's feelings?"

"Of course you may. I'll let her know you aren't feeling well. Do you want me to come with you?"

"No, ma'am. I'll be all right. I just have a splitting headache, and I think that if I go on—"

"I'll escort Julia home, Aunt Martha." Jake said from behind her. "I'll see her over and be back shortly."

"Thank you, Jake. I do believe she needs some rest."

Julia groaned silently. The last person she needed to have to speak to was Jake. "Really, I don't need an escort the few feet next door. I'm perfectly capable of going next door by myself."

"Perhaps, but I'm escorting you anyway," Jake said.

"I think that's a good idea, Julia. I'll check on you when I return, dear," Mrs. Heaton said.

"I'll be fine, really." She wanted Jake to hear the words as well as Mrs. Heaton. But as he took hold of her elbow when Mr. Tate opened the door for them, she realized she was the one who needed to hear them the most.

"Jake, this really is unnecessary," Julia said as soon as the door shut behind them.

"Perhaps for you, but it is necessary for me. I need to speak to you."

"Jake, I really don't feel well. Can it wait?"

"I—" He gazed into her eyes and let out a sigh. "I suppose so."

"Thank you. I just need to close my eyes and try to get rid of this headache."

"I understand. But I know you overheard mother telling everyone we'll be going back soon and I—"

"I am very happy for your sister, and I know your mother can't wait to get back home."

They were already back at Heaton House, and Jake opened the door for her. Then he turned her toward him. "I'm not ready to go back home, Julia. But—"

"You have to." She nodded. "I understand. And you need to go back next door or they'll all be wondering about us. Thank you again for coming after me today. I—" She looked up into his eyes.

"Julia, I don't care what they think next door. I thought I was going to lose you today, and I can't bear the thought—" He broke off and pulled her closer.

Before Julia could pull away, Jake bent his head and claimed her lips. It was the kind of kiss she'd only dreamed of, and Julia couldn't keep from responding.

And then she realized that she had. What was she thinking? What was he thinking? She pulled away. "Jake, no! Goodnight."

Then without waiting, Julia ran up the stairs to her room.

What had she done? There was no denying that she was totally in love with that cowboy. And he'd be leaving soon. How was she going to bear saying goodbye?

CHAPTER 14

$\mathcal{J}$ake had tossed and turned most of the night thinking about Julia. After he'd returned to the Walkers', he'd tried to join several conversations but soon lost interest when all he could think of was the woman next door.

And she was on his mind now as he hurried upstairs to breakfast, still thinking about the kiss they'd shared. For they had shared it.

He knew it wasn't a thank-you kiss just because he'd thought she was drowning and had gone to save her. And he knew Julia would never have responded the way she had if she didn't really care about him. Surely she wouldn't have.

He knew he'd been desperate to save her yesterday. That's when he knew he loved her. Wanted to court her. Wanted to marry her.

But even if Julia did feel the same way he did, would she be willing to leave her family and all she knew to be a rancher's wife? She'd said she'd dreamed of going out West for years, but she'd never gone. Still, she'd seemed open to visiting. But a visit was just that. There was an end point where one went back home, and he knew that whether he left her or she came and left there, he didn't want to be parted from her.

He hurried into the dining room, needing to see Julia, to have some idea of how she was feeling after that kiss. But his heart sank as he saw her chair was empty. "Has anyone checked on Julia this morning? Is she all right?"

"I believe she is. I popped over to check on her when I first got home last night, but she wasn't in her room. I thought perhaps she'd come down for some warm milk or something but found she'd left a note on my desk last night, Jake," Aunt Martha said. "She said not to worry as her headache had soon abated. She then had decided to go to her parents' home for the night so she could go to church with her family this morning."

"I don't remember her saying she'd be going away this weekend," Betsy said.

"I suppose she decided last minute. She has occasionally done that," Aunt Martha replied.

"But she hasn't in a long time," Emily said. "And it is odd that she'd go so suddenly without telling any of us."

"I believe she'll be home tonight or at least tomorrow. She probably just wanted to spend part of the holiday weekend with her family."

Jake could understand that she might. Still, that no one else knew that she might be going home for the day made Jake wonder if he'd ruined things with that kiss. Had he upset her so much that she left because she didn't want to see him again?

Well, he couldn't leave things as they were. But what was he going to do about it?

While at church, Jake tried to keep his mind on the sermon, which was about forgiveness, asking God for forgiveness, forgiving others, and asking those we've hurt in any way for forgiveness.

Somehow he felt as if he'd brought pain to Julia, although the last thing he'd ever want to do would be to hurt her. Had he insulted her or distressed her by kissing her when he was going to be leaving soon? If not, he'd certainly not acted the way he should have. And now she probably thought him no better than the cad who'd broken her heart years ago. Surely not. But how could he know?

Dear Lord, please don't let Julia think of me in that way. I love this woman. Please help me find a way to let her know how much that is and make this right. Please show me the way to her heart.

By the time the group arrived back home, Jake felt calmer. But he left right after Sunday dinner to go ride. It was the only way he could clear his mind, and there was no way he could stay at Heaton House just waiting for Julia to come back.

While the ride did clear his head enough to know that he missed Julia with every fiber of his being, his heart ached with the possibility that he'd hurt her. He had to know, had to find out, had to take some kind of action to convince her that he loved her. Even if she didn't feel the same way, he needed to let her know how he felt. He owed that to her—especially after that kiss.

He arrived back at Heaton House with a glimmer of a plan in mind. It was quiet except for the murmur of feminine voices coming from the study. He strode down the hall and knocked on the door before entering.

His mother and Aunt Martha smiled as he came into the room. "Jake, you've returned," his mother said. "I'm glad. I need to talk to you—"

"And I need to speak to you, Mother. I know you are eager to get back home, but I have things I need to take care of here as quickly as possible before I can even think of leaving. I'm in love with Julia, but I feel I may have messed everything up, and I'm asking for your and Aunt Martha's help."

"Finally!" Aunt Martha said. "We've suspected the two of you had fallen for each other but didn't want to interfere."

"Well, I need all the help I can get now."

"We've been waiting for you to ask, son. What do you need us to do?"

"Tell me if you really think I have a chance of convincing Julia to marry me and move out West."

"Well, as going out West was a dream she gave up on, you first must realize she'll be giving up a lot here to marry you and move out there," Aunt Martha said. "She'd be leaving a secure job and moving away from a family she loves."

"Not to mention the family she has here at Heaton House," his mother added. "It is a lot to ask, son."

Jake nodded. "I realize that. And I'm afraid she won't be able to do it."

"Well, perhaps you should think about what you're willing to give up for her," his mother said. "Once you have that figured out, you'll know what to do."

"And Jake," his aunt said, "for what it's worth, I've watched you two together, and I do believe she cares deeply for you."

Suddenly Jake knew exactly what to do. "Thank you. You've helped more than you know." He kissed them both on their cheeks. For the first time since Julia had run upstairs the evening before, his heart filled with hope and he had a plan.

AFTER CHURCH AND SUNDAY DINNER, Julia's siblings had all scattered—the boys to play stick ball with the neighbors and her sisters to visit their friend next door. While Julia's papa was enjoying his Sunday afternoon nap, her mother brewed them pot of tea. After they'd settled at the kitchen table, Julia's mother finally confronted her as Julia had known she would.

"All right, Julia, I've been waiting for you to tell me why you came home at bedtime last night."

"I told you I just missed you all and— "

"Julia, I'm your mama. I know something has happened to

sadden you. I can see it in your eyes and even hear it in your voice." She poured their tea. "Now, tell me what it is."

"I'm afraid I've fallen in love with Jake, Mama."

"But that's wonderful! And it's not news to me. I could see how you two were headed that way when you brought him to visit. We've just been waiting for you to tell us."

"It's *not* wonderful, Mama. His mother is ready to go back home to Oklahoma, and I can't bear the thought of his leaving, especially since I don't really know how he feels about me." The tears she'd been holding back since the moment Jake's mother had announced that they needed to get back home suddenly broke loose and began to run down her face.

Her mother enveloped her in a hug and handed her a napkin to wipe her tears. "But dear, we know he loves you. We saw it when you brought him to visit. And if that hadn't convinced us, the beef he sent us certainly convinced your papa of his intentions."

"He sent you some of his beef?"

"Yes, we assumed you knew. It was quite delicious. I had enough to make us a roast that gave us two meals, and then there was the stew meat you ate today."

Jake had sent her parents beef and had never mentioned it.

"Did he send a note or anything?"

"Yes, he said it was to thank us for our hospitality and that it came from cattle in Oklahoma. He also mentioned that he treasured his friendship with you."

"Do you still have that note?"

"Of course we do," her papa said from the doorway. He obviously had awakened. "I'll go and get it."

Julia looked at her mother. "How long has he been standing there? Did he hear everything?"

"Possibly. I'm sure he woke up and came when he heard you crying."

"So he knows how I feel about Jake?"

Her father walked back into the room and handed her the note Jake had sent them. "Yes, I do."

Julia read the precise masculine handwriting, and it brought tears to her eyes once more. "How kind he is. He tried to save my life yesterday. Only there was no need, but—"

"Save your life? What happened?"

Julia explained to them about floating out so far and then trying to dislodge the seaweed, causing the boarders to think she was in trouble. Then Jake had pulled her up out of the water.

"And, from what he said and the look in his eyes, I thought that he might care about me the way I care about him.

"Then we got back to Heaton House, and his mother had just received a letter from his sister telling her she would be a grand-mother come the new year. Now she wants to get back there as soon as she can and—" Julia grabbed the napkins once more to stem her tears. "I don't want him to go!"

"Oh, daughter." Her papa pulled a chair up close and hugged her, rocking her back and forth as he'd done when she was young. "Dry your tears, child. I can almost guarantee you that your Jake doesn't want to leave you any more than you want him to. It was plain as day how he feels about you when we first met him. And how you feel about him. Have you not talked since his mother mentioned leaving?"

"Well, he wanted to." She wasn't sure she wanted to tell her parents about the kiss that told her how much he cared and the fact that her response must have told him the same about how she felt. It was something she'd treasure forever. But he was leaving and he hadn't actually told her, and she—

"And why didn't he? Did you stop him, Julia?" her mother asked.

"I—yes, I did. I wanted to hear but was afraid it wouldn't be what I wanted him to say, and then even if it was, I'm not sure I'm ready to—" She broke off and shook her head. "I ran upstairs. Then later I came here."

"What are you afraid of, daughter? Why are you afraid to live your dream?"

"Mama, I don't want to leave you all here. What if you get sick again? Or Papa—"

"Daughter, you can't live your life worrying about us," her mother replied. "And you can't use us as an excuse not to choose the life you long for, no matter how frightened you are of the outcome."

"But—"

"No buts. We will always be here for you no matter what," her father insisted.

"You've always had a habit of running from things that frighten you, Julia," Her mother said. "At least until you've thought them over."

"Have I?"

"Yes, you have," her mother said. "And what I suggest you do now, daughter, is a lot of soul searching and praying, asking the Lord to guide you in this."

"And remember, you are stronger than you believe you are," Papa said. "You are our child. You seem to have forgotten that we left our country and our families to begin a new life here together. Do you think we weren't afraid of the outcome? But we'd do it all over again, wouldn't we, Mama?"

"We would. Julia, the Lord did not give you a spirit of timidity. You've always been a strong woman. But you can't live your life afraid of being hurt. At some point, you must trust the Lord and your heart. Go to Him for guidance, to figure out what it is your heart wants. And when you know, you need to return to Heaton House and have the courage to listen to Jake. You owe him that."

Her mother was right. And now Julia realized how childish she'd acted. She'd been hurt once, and the Lord had helped her through it. He was there for her now, no matter what the outcome was. "You're right, I do need to figure it all out. I'm going for a walk in the park. I'll go back later."

"I'm sure Jake won't be leaving until after Independence Day. He's probably as confused as you are. Stay tonight and go back tomorrow morning," Julia's mother said. "Hopefully that will give you time to work it all out in your mind so that you know what you want to say when you speak with Jake."

Julia hugged them both before heading downstairs. They were right. She needed time alone with the Lord. It was past time to give it all to Him and trust Him to guide her in what to do.

CHAPTER 15

*T*he next morning, Julia felt more at peace than she had in years. She'd done much praying and soul-searching the night before and had finally realized that being truly independent meant having to make hard choices on her own, not making excuses so that she didn't have to.

It was Independence Day, and she was going to finally be independent. Oh, she'd told herself she was for years, but she'd only been fooling herself. Moving over to Gramercy Park from Brooklyn hadn't made her independent. Neither had being able to help her parents out from time to time. Nor had being promoted at work and making a better wage.

Something had always held her back from doing the things she'd dreamed of—moving out West, having an adventure, and trusting her heart to another. And that something was her. Her own fears and timidity had held her back from being free to follow the Lord's plan for her life.

She'd wanted to be in control so much that she'd said no to herself. Still, the Lord's timing was always right, and He'd brought Jake Tucker into her life. If what she thought and hoped for didn't happen, then He'd help her deal with it.

But she had to take a chance. Had to know how Jake felt about her and even had to let him know how she felt about him. There was no reason to hide her feelings from him. If he didn't feel the same way, she'd get over it. Someday. But she had to live this life the Lord had given her. She couldn't continue to let it glide by, watching first one and then another of her friends reach out and grab happiness while she hung back, telling herself she was content with what she had.

Well, that was over. She might have to settle for less than her dreams, but not without trying to reach them. She headed back to Heaton House with her parents' blessings. They wanted her to be happy no matter where it took her.

Heaton House was quiet when Julia went inside, and she wondered if everyone had left for the parade already. But just as she reached the staircase, Mrs. Heaton came out of her study.

As soon as she saw Julia, her smile was wide and welcoming.

"Julia, dear. I'm so glad you made it home in time for the parade! The girls went to freshen up and Lucy and I are just waiting for them to come down."

At least Jake's mother was still here, and if so, then he was, too. But Julia didn't want to ask about him. She had to bide her time, but before this day was over, she was going to let Jake Tucker know how much she loved him and find out how he felt about her.

"Then I'd better get my things upstairs and change so I don't make you all late."

"Don't rush, we won't leave without you. The men have already gone to find us a spot. And we won't be having our picnic this afternoon. Michael has said we can all go up to the rooftop of his building to watch the fireworks tonight, and we're going to have our dinner there. He said he didn't know why we haven't done that before now, but we're all really looking forward to it. So, dress up a bit this evening. Everyone thought it would be fun to do so."

"That does sound nice, and the view will be spectacular from up there," Julia said. The thought of seeing fireworks going off all over the city, especially if she could see them with Jake, was exciting. If he'd be beside her.

But even if not, she was determined to look on the bright side. And if she kept that kiss in mind, there was no reason not to.

❦

THE WOMEN WERE on the way downstairs and seemed glad to see her. The only mention of her abrupt departure came from Betsy.

"Why didn't you let us know you were going to spend time with your family, Julia? They are all right, aren't they?"

"Yet, they're fine. I'm sorry if I worried you."

Julia set her bag in her room and hurried to change into what she'd planned to wear to the picnic. She added a broad brimmed hat to protect her from the sun and quickly joined the others downstairs.

Jake's mother greeted her as if she'd missed her and Julia could only hope that her son had too.

The women headed out to the hack Michael had sent to pick them up and the driver took them over to Fifth Avenue and Broadway where they found Michael and Jake waiting for them.

Jake's gaze found hers, and for a moment she forgot to breathe and she thought her heart had stopped beating. It felt as if she hadn't seen him in weeks or months instead of a couple of days. She drank in the sight of him as he approached her.

He smiled as he reached her. "Julia, I'm glad you returned in time to celebrate the day with us."

Julia released a silent sigh. His words were enough to let her know that he would still speak to her. "I'm glad I made it back, too. I'm looking forward to the parade and the fireworks this evening."

"It's going to be great. After the parade, I'm going to help Michel set things up on the rooftop of his building.

And she prayed they'd get a chance to speak to each other in private at some point this evening. She might come away from the conversation heartbroken, but she had to know how he felt about her, and she desperately wanted to know as soon as possible.

"We're just down in the next block," Michael said, leading his mother as Jake took the arm his mother held out to him. He glanced over at Julia and she hoped it was disappointment she was seeing in his eyes as he looked back at her. *Dear Lord, please give us a chance to talk before this day is over.*

She smiled at Jake and fell into step with Betsy and Emily. When they arrived at the place Dave and Stephen had held for them, she was pleased to find that Rebecca, Ben and Jenny were there as well. But happy as she was to see Millicent and Matt along with Elizabeth and John join them, she had a feeling getting a private word in with Jake was going to be impossible— at least during the parade.

However, it didn't keep them from stealing glances at each other in between marching bands. They all waved at Cole as he rode down the street with other members of the mounted police, as they followed the dignitaries. There were colorful floats interspersed in between it all, with clowns doing summersaults along the way.

❀

IT'D BEEN a busy day for Jake, and he couldn't wait to get back to Heaton House and get ready for the party that evening. When Julia had showed up at the parade, Jake had never been happier to see anyone in his life. Ever.

He'd barely noticed the parade, his mind on how to convince her of his love, praying that she felt the same way and that he would be able to get her to himself so that he could find out. He was stepping out in faith that everything would work out, knowing that one way or another the Lord would be with him.

For the last few hours, he and Michael had been setting up tables and chairs on the rooftop of the Heaton building in preparation for the meal Aunt Martha was bringing over and watching the fireworks later.

"You're awfully quiet, Jake. Anything you'd like to talk about?" Michael asked.

"I just have a lot on my mind."

"Couldn't be anything like Julia's action to the news that you might be leaving soon the other night, could it?"

"What do you know about it?"

"Jake, I saw the look on her face when your mother told everyone that you and she would be leaving soon. And you two couldn't take your eyes off each other at the parade today. I believe Julia's fallen in love with you."

Hope flooded Jake's heart. "Do you?"

"I do. And I'd hate to see her hurt. She has reason not to trust men very much."

"I know. She told me about it and that you saved her from making a horrible mistake."

"She told you about that cad?"

"Yes."

"Then she holds you in very high regard. As far as I know, the only people who know anything about that time in her life are my mother and I, and perhaps her mother and father. But I'm not sure she's told even them. Jake, Julia is like another sister to me, and I don't want to see her hurt. You'd best not be toying with her affections."

"Michael, I love the woman and want to ask her to be my wife. But she's been at her parents since the night of Georgia's party. All I want is a chance to tell her and find out if she might feel the same way."

"She does care about you, Jake," Michael said. "I know Julia well, and I'm sure she's afraid of what she feels for you--if she can trust her judgment. But we've all noticed how you two are around each other. It's seemed obvious to anyone but the two of you. And after today, I don't see how either of you could try to deny it."

"Well, I thought she did care, especially after a kiss we shared that night before she went home. I tried to tell her then, but she ran upstairs and then she left and I haven't seen her since."

"She let you kiss her?"

"I don't know that she let me, but she did respond."

"Jake, Julia wouldn't have let you get away with kissing her and especially not respond, if she didn't care deeply for you. But if she ran off, it tells me that she needs assurance of some kind. You've got to tell her how you feel, and don't put it off. She needs to know how much you love her."

"I don't intend to delay. I'm hoping to get her to myself tonight for long enough to be able to let her know how I feel about her. Getting time together isn't easy to do."

Michael nodded. "I can see how that might be difficult at the boardinghouse."

They put the last few chairs around the tables. Then Michael looked over at him with a grin. "Jake, here's an idea. Why don't you and Julia get stuck in the elevator on purpose sometime this evening?"

"On purpose?"

"Yes, I'll show you how you can stop the elevator and restart it. You'll have to find a way to get her in the elevator so that it's just the two of you in there. Then you should be able to say whatever you need to."

"And how am I going to get her to get in the elevator with me? I don't know that she'll even talk to me with everyone around."

"Maybe you could simply say you need to talk to her in private."

"That might work, Michael. She knows that I want to speak to her, and I'm praying she wants to hear what I have to say. But if not, I think I can depend on your mother and mine to help me."

Michael chuckled. "Then it should all work out just fine. And for extra assurance, I'll be praying it does." He slapped Jake on the back. "She's a good woman, and you'll be a blessed man to have her for a wife. But I can think of no one else I believe would be as good for her as you will be."

"Thank you, Michael. That means a lot to me. But first I've got to find out how she feels about me."

"Well, let's get going so we can get back here and you can find out."

By the time Jake got back to Heaton House, his hopes were high, but as he walked in the door and remembered how she'd run from him on Saturday night, his memories lowered his expectations. She might care about him as Michael had insisted. She might even love him. But that didn't mean she was willing to trust him—or herself.

Well, he wouldn't know until he asked, and that wouldn't happen unless he could get her alone. He headed down to his aunt's study to find her and his mother having a cup of tea.

"Jake, I'm so glad Julia did come back in time for the parade and festivities tonight," his mother said. "Have you had a chance to talk to her?

"Not yet. Michael and I have come up with a plan of sorts, but I think I could use your help in carrying it through."

His aunt motioned for him to take a seat. "Tell us what you need."

JULIA DIDN'T THINK she'd ever been more nervous in her life as she dressed for the party that evening. She couldn't wait to see Jake again, while at the same time she feared she'd misread the looks they'd exchanged at the parade and that he might not want to talk to her as much as she wanted to speak to him.

But she had to find out where they stood. Did he want them to still be friends, or what? They'd talked about corresponding after he went back home, but after that kiss they'd shared she wasn't sure she could continue on as if it hadn't occurred.

That was not a friendly kiss on the cheek. No, the kiss they'd shared had filled her thoughts all weekend. And so, had the expression in his eyes when she'd broken the kiss and pulled out of his arms.

He'd wanted to talk to her, but she didn't give him a chance because she knew he'd soon be leaving and she couldn't bear the thought of it. But bear it or not, she had to deal with it.

She put on a lightweight dress made of blue-and-white dotted Swiss. Then she put her hair up with a blue ribbon to match. She loved this holiday and seeing fireworks displays that shot beautiful lights up into the sky. It'd be wonderful to see them from up high.

She took a deep breath before leaving her room. *Dear Lord, please guide me tonight and help me to know what to do.* She met up with Betsy as she left her room, and the two went downstairs together.

"I am so glad you're back. Jake wasn't the same while you were gone."

"What do you mean?"

"He looked miserable. Did something happen between you two before you left so suddenly?"

Betsy had no qualms about being forthright. But Julia wasn't going to tell her about the kiss. It was too special and if Jake didn't feel about her the way she felt about him, she didn't want everyone at Heaton House to feel sorry for her. The Lord would help her through it, and so would her family and Mrs. Heaton, if need be. But she didn't want the pity of everyone else if she were to remain a spinster forever. "Why would you think that?"

"I don't know. I—"

"Wait up, you two," Emily said from the top of the staircase. "I am so excited about this evening, aren't you? And Julia, I'm so glad you made it back in time to celebrate the day with us. I hope all is well with your family."

"They're fine and I'm glad I was able to spend part of the holiday weekend with them."

Just as they reached the parlor, the sounds of men's firm foot-steps could be heard coming up from downstairs. Her heart fluttered in anticipation of seeing Jake again. She heard the rumble of his voice and turned to see him enter the room along with the rest of the male boarders.

As he his gaze caught hers and then moved to her lips, she caught her breath. Oh, how she loved that man.

CHAPTER 16

*J*ake's heart filled to near overflowing as he captured Julia's gaze. He loved this woman with all his heart, and he could not leave this city without finding out where he stood with her. Wasn't sure he could leave it without *her*.

The look in her eyes as he'd walked into the parlor had given him a glimmer of hope, but it could be wishful thinking on his part. Still, either way, he was going to find out tonight. "Will you sit with me for dinner?"

"I—"

"Men, would you mind helping Gretchen and Maida get the baskets loaded into the hack? It's here to pick them up." His aunt interrupted whatever Julia had been about to say. "Their beaus are meeting us there, and they're going to set everything up for us and then join us for the festivities."

Jake smiled at Julia and shook his head, wanting to hear what she'd been about to say, but he was needed elsewhere. He knew she understood.

He and the other men helped carry out the baskets of food Gretchen and Maida had prepared, and he was pleased to see that

158

they were excited as well. The two women were quite happy that they'd be joining them for the meal and the fireworks show afterwards. It said a lot for both his aunt and her boarders that even the servants felt a part of her family.

He'd miss all of them when he went back to Oklahoma. But even if things didn't work out the way he prayed they would tonight, he'd be back. He had family here, and he did business here. And he couldn't bear the thought of never seeing Julia again.

The men saw the maids off and went back in to Heaton House where his aunt immediately called everyone together. They'd be going by trolley to the building.

"All right everyone, let's go. The others will meet us there," Aunt Martha said.

"The others?" Julia asked.

"All our former boarders have been invited," Emily said.

"Wonderful!" Julia said.

"The more the merrier," Jake managed, only he wasn't sure more people were going to make it easier for him to get Julia to himself. He'd asked his mother and aunt to try to help him, but they hadn't told him what they'd come up with or even if they'd come up with anything, yet.

The sun was beginning to lower in the sky as they left Heaton House for Michael's office building, and everyone seemed to be in festive moods. The American flag outside Heaton House reminded them of the reason for their celebration as they headed toward the trolley stop.

Jake wanted to sit by Julia, but by the time he got on, the seat beside her was taken by Betsy, and Emily took the one across from them. Stephen quickly slipped in beside her, leaving Jake and Joe to take the one behind them, while his mother and aunt shared the one directly across from him and Joe. He couldn't even ask if they'd come up with a plan because everyone would hear.

It was a quick trip to the stop nearest the Heaton building, and the former boarders all began arriving right after they did. They all greeted each other as part of a family as they entered the building and headed toward the elevators.

As Julia was the last one on the first elevator, Jake's hopes that they might end up on the same one sank, but he wasn't going to give up. Finally, he decided to relax and leave it all in the Lord's hands. He'd see that Jake had some time with Julia.

As they got to the top floor, the elevator opened and then they went up steps that led to a door that opened out onto the rooftop. There was a three-foot brick ledge around the rooftop to keep anyone from falling off, and the view was priceless. There were a few buildings on the street that were taller than this one, but the ones across the street were not, and they could see out to the East River where there were sure to be some fireworks set off. They'd be able to have a full view.

"This is wonderful, Michael," Julia said. "Why have we not been up here before?"

Michael chuckled. "I truly never thought of it until Violet mentioned it. It's the perfect spot, isn't it?"

"It certainly is," his mother said. "And I'm glad you thought of getting candles for the tables. That will make our dinner even more special."

"And I see we even have place cards," Rebecca said. "Who thought of that?"

"Violet again, on both the candles and the nameplates," Michael answered.

"I should have known, brother mine. I couldn't imagine you thinking of it yourself. But then I don't think Ben would have either."

Her husband chuckled. "You're absolutely right. But it is a nice touch."

"It'll be especially nice once it gets dark," Violet said behind him. She was holding baby Marcus who reached out to his papa.

"Are we ready to eat, Mother?" Michael asked, taking his son from his wife and kissing his cheek.

"We are. Please announce that everything is ready and say a blessing for us before everyone begins to fix their plates."

Michael got everyone's attention by clinking a spoon against one of the glasses on the table next to him.

"Everyone, we're about ready to eat. We're to help ourselves to the buffet and sit where my lovely wife put your place cards. But first, please pray with me."

As his guests did as requested, Michael began to pray. "Dear Father, we come before You so very thankful for this day, that we are able to worship You in freedom. We thank You for the family and friends who are celebrating with us. We thank You for our many blessings and for the food we are about to eat. In Jesus' name, amen."

"Let's find our spots first," Julia suggested, and Jake was happy to oblige. If a card with his name on it wasn't at the same table as Julia's, he was going to do some quick switching. It was at the second table that they found their cards right next to each other. Michael must have mentioned how Jake felt about Julia to his wife, and if this was the result, he was quite happy that he did.

❀

JULIA LAID DOWN HER PURSE, and they made their way to the line that'd formed at the tables that were loaded down with all kinds of picnic fare. There was fried chicken and a glazed ham, creamed potatoes and sweet potatoes, along with macaroni and pea salads and all manner of side dishes. There were pies--apple, peach, and cherry—and coconut and chocolate cakes.

"What a spread this is," Jake said from behind Julia as he began to help himself.

"It certainly is," she agreed as she placed a small slice of ham and a chicken wing on her plate. They made their way along the buffet and went back to their table to find that Millicent and Matt were already seated, as were Elizabeth and John with baby John William asleep in a stroller beside them.

Georgia and Sir Tyler were seated at a table with her parents and Jake's mother, along with Mrs. Heaton. Sir Tyler's girls, Lillie and Polly, were seated at a smaller table nearby with Jenny and looked to be having a wonderful time.

Julia looked around to see that baby Marcus was in a high-chair Michael and Violet must have brought from home, and Rebecca and Ben were at their table.

The present boarders were spread out among the tables as were Gretchen and Maida and their gentlemen friends. It was so good to see everyone she'd boarded with for so long all in one place again. Julia did love living at Heaton House.

As people got up to get dessert, Julia could see Gretchen hurrying over to Mrs. Heaton at the next table, a worried expression on her face.

"Don't worry about it, Gretchen. I should have thought of it. I'll take care of it now."

Then Mrs. Heaton rushed over to their table. "Jake, we forgot the ice-cream! I know it's an imposition, but I hate to ask Gretchen or Maida since they have their beaus here--"

"There's no need to do that. I'll be glad to go get it."

"It's been kept in containers on ice in the icebox. And there are some towels and baskets." She turned to Julia. "Would you mind going with him, Julia? You know where things are and—"

"Of course I'll go help him find everything, Mrs. Heaton." Julia scooted back her chair and grabbed her purse. Maybe this would give her and Jake a chance to have a private conversation at last.

"Thank you both!" Then she hurried back to her table, a look of relief on her face.

"Before you go," Millicent said, "I have something for you. I've brought everyone some of the photos I took at the Statue of Liberty. I'll give you two yours now in case you want to leave them at Heaton House." She pulled two packets from her bag and handed them each one.

"Thank you so much, Millicent. I can't wait to see them."

"We can look at them on the way to Heaton House." Jake took her arm. "We'll be back."

He led her to the stairs and then to the elevator. The door had barely closed before he turned to her. "Julia, I—" Suddenly Jake wasn't sure what to say, how to say it and he quickly changed the subject. "Let's look at the photographs Millicent gave us!"

Julia's heart did a nose dive. Now that they had even a moment alone, she'd hoped they were finally going to have a real talk. But evidently, Jake wasn't as eager to get things settled between them as she was. Trying to hide her dismay, she quickly opened the packet Millicent had handed her and pulled out the photographs. "Jake, how did she get these shots?"

One was of him and Julia in front of the statue, and several others were of them inside the crown beside several windows. But she'd caught them smiling at each other instead of out at her. And then there was one just of Jake, but he was looking down at Julia, and the expression in his eyes was there for all to see. He did care about her.

She looked over at Jake who'd opened his packet and saw him pull his photos out and look them over before his eyes met hers. "Julia, we have to talk."

"Yes, we do."

"We'll talk at Heaton House."

"But we have to—"

Everyone can wait a little longer for their ice cream."

Julia smiled. He did want to settle things. "All right.

Jake nodded just as the elevator stopped. At the lobby, its doors opened, and they rushed outside. In only moments, Jake had hailed a cab and helped her in. Then they were on their way to Heaton House.

"Do we have the same photos?" he asked.

"I don't know."

They looked at each other's photos to find that they were the same ones, except for the single shots, and those differed only that Jake's was one of her with the same kind of expression in her eyes as he had in his on Julia's photo. Their gazes sought each other just as the hack pulled up at Heaton House.

Julia's heart skipped a beat as he helped her out of the vehicle. He paid the driver and they hurried up the steps of Heaton House. It seemed unnaturally quiet inside. And very . . . private.

Jake turned to her and lightly grasped her arms. Julia's pulse shot through her veins and her heart hammered against her chest as he turned her toward him.

"Julia, I am not leaving for Oklahoma until we get things straightened out between us."

"I'm glad. But—"

Jake silenced her with the touch of his fingertips to her lips. "Please, hear me out. I feel I must apologize for my actions the other night. I acted on impulse and broke the rules of propriety, and well, all I can say is that I would do it all over again for my intentions were and are honorable toward you. I may be leaving to escort mother back home, but I *will* be coming back, as soon as I can."

Her heart filled with joy at his words. He wasn't apologizing for the kiss. He'd do it again and he was coming back!

"I love you, Julia. I think I began to fall in love with you the very first time I held you in my arms and looked into your beautiful eyes. But I fought it as long as I could. I didn't want to fall in love again. Only I don't think I knew what real love was. I've certainly never felt like this before. I can't bear to think of not sharing my days with you and hearing about yours. I want to see you every morning and kiss you goodnight every night. I have to know if you could ever love me back." Only then did he remove his fingertips from her lips.

"Oh, Jake. I am so sorry I ran out on you the other night. I was just so confused. The thought of your going home was more than I could deal with at the time, and then you kissed me and I—"

"Kissed me back."

The expression in his eyes had her smiling and nodding her head. "Yes, I did. And because of that, you must know that I love you, too."

At her admission, Jake tipped her face to his and bent to repeat the kiss she hadn't been able to get out of her mind. Only this time it was more than she'd ever dreamed it could be and left her in no doubt that he loved her just as much as she loved him.

Julia wasn't sure who ended the kiss, but Jake tilted her face up so that they gazed into each other's eyes. "I know it won't be easy for you to leave your family and friends here, and I do understand that. But if you'll marry me, we can stay here. I've talked to Captain Marlow, and he told me I could have a job on the Mounted Police Division anytime I want it. I'm willing to come back to stay if you can't bear to leave. Will you marry me?"

"Jake, I can't ask you to give up your ranch. You've worked very hard to make it a success, and I won't ask you to give it up."

"I can sell out to my brother-in-law."

The enormity of what he was willing to do took her breath away. "No, Jake, I can't let you do that."

The expression in his eyes told her that he thought she was refusing him, so she hurried to assure him nothing could be further from the truth. "But, yes! I will marry you. I will be honored to become your wife."

"You will?" His voice was deep and husky, and her heart felt as if it would burst. "You'll move out West with me?"

"I will. How can I not when you've offered to give up so much for me? Besides, I'm ready for an adventure, and I can't think of anything more exciting than becoming a rancher's wife —your wife."

Jake picked her up and swung her around. "I promise you we'll come back on a regular basis so that you can see your family. And they're welcome to come see us anytime. I want to keep in contact with my family, too, and hopefully do more business in the city. We'll be coming back often. I love you, Julia."

"And I love you, Jake. I think I've loved you from the moment you caught me that first night. And this time, I know I can trust my judgement where you are concerned."

"You can trust me always and forever." They shared a kiss that sealed their promises to each other and then Julia reluctantly pulled away.

"We'd best get the ice cream. They'll be wondering what's keeping us." She captured his hand and pulled him toward the kitchen.

Jake chuckled as he followed her. "I'm pretty sure some of them might have an idea, but I suppose you're right."

Julia blushed at the thought that others might know how she felt about Jake, but then she smiled realizing they would all soon know how they felt about each other.

They quickly wrapped the two ice-cream containers in towels that'd been left out for that purpose and put them in baskets for easier carrying. Then they hurried out to the waiting hack.

"I hope it doesn't melt before we get there," Julia said.

"Neither do I."

"I hope we get there before the fireworks begin," Julia said.

"Oh, I think they might already have begun," Jake said.

The expression in his eyes sent her pulse racing, and Julia was had a feeling he was right.

❦

WHEN THEY ARRIVED at Michael's building, they hurried the ice-cream into the elevator.

Jake set down the baskets and pushed the switch to take them to the top floor, then as they stopped at the top floor, he pulled Julia into his arms once more. He kissed her, leaning against the elevator switches and somehow putting it into motion again. They both laughed and kissed as they rode it down and back up again.

Then the doors opened and they hurried up the stairs to the rooftop. Jake opened the door and hurried to set out the ice-cream.

"About time you got back! I was about to come looking for you," Michael said.

"Yes we thought you'd forgotten about us," Betsy said.

But they both grinned as everyone begin to fall in line while Gretchen and Maida began to dish the ice cream up.

Jake leaned down and whispered into Julia's ear. "I suppose we should tell them our news."

"Yes, we should."

"I'll wait until they've all been served and then get their attention.

"All right."

Julia and Jake waited at the back of the line until everyone else had been served and then, after they took their bowls of the treat, they headed back to the table they'd been setting at. Once Gretchen and Maida joined their beaus with their own ice-cream, Jake stood and tapped on the side of his bowl with his spoon.

"Everyone, I'd like to make an announcement." He looked down at Julia and then took her hand in his and drew her up to stand beside him. "As several of you might have noticed, Julia and I were not in a big hurry to get back with the ice cream. But there is a very good reason for that. I took advantage of the time alone to propose to Julia. And she accepted."

The congratulations and laughter told them both and they all *did* have an idea what might be holding them up! Jake's mother and Mrs. Heaton were the first to come give them a hug.

"I was hoping our idea to leave the ice cream behind would work!" his aunt said.

"It was the only thing we could come up with," Jake's mother said.

"And it worked beautifully," Jake said. They received congratulations from the others until a loud boom captured everyone's attention.

"Jake, look!" Julia pointed out over the rooftop. "Isn't it beautiful?"

"Oh yes, but nowhere nearly as beautiful as you!" With everyone's attention on the fireworks, he stole a quick kiss, and Julia's heart filled with so much love the beat of it seemed to mirror the bursting flares of sound, light, and colors that broke over the rooftop and seemed to shower down over them. All she could think of was how blessed she was as she thanked the Lord above for turning long lost dreams into a beautiful reality.

ABOUT THE AUTHOR

Bestselling author Janet Lee Barton is a Romantic Times Book of the Year winner as well as a multiple ACFW Carol Award nominee. Janet was born in New Mexico and has lived all over the South. She and her husband now call Oklahoma home and have recently downsized to a condo, which they love. When Janet isn't writing or reading, she loves to cook for family, work in her small garden, travel and sew. She writes both Historical and Contemporary romance, and loves writing about faith, families, friends—and of course—falling in love.

Visit her at: www.janetleebarton.com. Click on the Stormy's Rainbow cover to sign up for her newsletter and get writing news first.

Book List
  Novellas
  Harvest of Love
  The Cookie Jar
  Language of Love
  Novels
  (New Mexico Series - historical)
  (The novella, Harvest of Love series)
  A Promise Made
  A Place Called Home
  Making Amends

Three-in-one: New Mexico
(New Mexico Series - Contemporary)
Family Circle
Family Ties
Family Reunion
Three-in-one: New Mexico Weddings
(Arkansas Series - Historical)
A Love For Keeps
A Love All Her Own
A Love to Cherish
Three-in-one: Brides of Arkansas
(Mississippi Series-Contemporary)
Unforgettable
To Love Again
With Open Arms
Three-in One: Mississippi Weddings
(Oklahoma Series-Historical)
I'd Sooner Have Love
Sooner Sunrise
Sooner Sunset
Three-in-One: Land Run Brides
Other Historical Novels:
Stirring Up Romance
Remedy For Love
Love Calling
(Golden Creek Contemporary Series)
Stormy's Rainbow (Book 1)
To Heal A Cowboy's Heart (Book 2)
Love Inspired Historical's
(Boardinghouse Betrothal Series)
Somewhere To Call Home
A Place of Refuge
Home For Her Heart- (Romantic Times Book of the Year Award)

A Daughter's Return

The Mistletoe Kiss

A Nanny For Keeps

And a continuation of the **Boardinghouse Betrothals** series in new stories which will be coming out under the series name of **Heaton House.**

The Cowboy and The Lady is the first of these. There will also be **Heaton House Companion Stories**, too. I'm very excited to continue my New York City Historicals.

To connect with Janet

www.janetleebarton.com

janetbwrites@gmail.com

Made in the USA
Lexington, KY
21 August 2017